Larame

The Death and Life

of

Larame Crighton

Written by

Bob Richey

TWISTED TRUTH
PRESS

Published by:

Book Cover by ZsaZsa

Illustrations by Zsa Zsa -   ZsaZsa@Zsa--Zsa.com

ISBN –978-1-970990-16-4   Paperback

First edition 2025

Dedication

This book is dream inspired. I listened to Larame dictate it night after night in my dreams.

I dedicate this book to the few who believe and understand. Some have also lived this experience. Get up and write down what your spirit requests. They may ask, beg, or command, but it's our responsibility to follow our dreams.

To everyone else, follow your dreams too, wherever they may lead you.

Enjoy!

Larame

Preface

This book was dream inspired. To most people that means I dreamed it up in my head. That's only partially true. While all of the writings in this book are original, and I wrote it completely without anyone's help or assistance, I can't count out the cowboy, long ago dead, that inspires me to write his story. Larame Crighton, (he spelled it out to me, but if it's spelled wrong, for gosh sakes, I was asleep at the time,) is the one that tells this story from the grave. I could just take all the credit for any of the good things echoing through this book, but alas, he still visits me in my dreams. Believe what you will, I'm just following my dreams wherever they may lead.

Enjoy!

The Death and Life

Of

Larame Crighton

Index

Ch. 01 – Page 1   Dying's Not Easy

Ch. 02 – Page 9   You Stay Dead

Ch. 03 – Page 19   Here Lies Larame Crighton

Ch. 04 – Page 25   One Scream Leads to Another

Ch. 05 – Page 33   Heaven and Hell

Ch. 06 – Page 47   Tell it to the Judge

Ch. 07 – Page 65   Ducks all Lined Up in a Row

Ch. 08 – Page 81   Buddy Collins

Ch. 09 – Page 97   The Show's a-Just Start'in

Ch. 10 – Page 103   Save the Safe

Ch. 11 – Page 115   Star

Ch. 12 – Page 135   Here Comes the Judge

Ch. 13 – Page 143   From Good to Bad to Good

Ch. 14 – Page 155   A Dream Come True

Ch. 15 – Page 171   Lefty

Ch. 16 – Page 181   Yuma, Center of the Southwest

Ch. 17 – Page 189   Diary of a Young Outlaw

Ch. 18 – Page 199   New Orleans

Ch. 19 – Page 211   Rose

Ch. 20 – Page 217   Cliff Williams

Larame

"Yer a goner," Cliff told him. "God damn it, your boot knows you're a goner, your shirt knows you're a goner, even the little fucking bird knows your time's up."

Larame

Chapter 1

Dying's Not Easy

Our story begins at the end. Larame Crighton lay on the hot desert sand clutching the hole in his only good shirt. The red blotch around the hole told most of the story, and the desert sand showing a growing large pool of dark blood under him told the rest.

Larame looked up at Cliff, who was still on his horse.

"Help me back up on Star," he pleaded.

From his vantage point, Cliff could see a hole worn into the bottom of Larame's boot. He looked at his friend's hat laying a few feet from his head and noticed a small bird place a piece of straw inside the upside-down hat.

"Yer a goner," Cliff told him. "God damn it, your boot knows you're a goner, your shirt knows you're a goner, even the little fucking bird knows your time's up."

He paused and then continued, "Seems you're the only one here that doesn't know it."

"I gotta get now!" he scowled, "don't be thinking I stole your horse. Star has been following me and Spank fer months now, and I don't reckon he's gonna quit anytime soon."

"Your only chance is if the posse comes soon and treats you right, but I doubt that's gonna happen. Yer gonna be dead before they get here."

"If it means anything, you were a good friend and I'll miss you and I hate leaving you like this but, I gotta go now!"

"Gid-up!" he yelled, and spurred Spank into a full run. To his surprise, Star stayed at Larame's side.

True to Cliff's word, the posse arrived too late to help him. The desert sun and heat had pulled the last bit of life out of Larame Crighton's body.

It took three of the deputies to hoist him face down on Star's back, and the position showed the enormity of the wound. The blood caked back of his shirt and on the top of his jeans showed more dried blood than a man can stand to lose. One of the deputies proceeded to lead Star and the dead outlaw back to Yuma.

The rest of the posse rode hard to catch Cliff Williams, believed to be responsible for a string of misdoings in Yuma. They wanted him, and rode hard to arrest him, but spirits started to sink when they realized he had slowly changed directions and was now headed south towards Mexico.

Just inside the Mexican border up ahead, there was a Christian mission, and they would help anyone crossing the border if they gave themselves to Christ. If Cliff made it there, he was home-free. He knew this was true because he had done it before.

Riding through the moonlit night, he reached the mission, accepted Christ as his Lord and Savior again, and headed south into Mexico. The three hundred dollars from the bank would allow him to live like a king for the next few years.

Back at Yuma, Larame was yanked off his horse Star by Joe, the undertaker. Star would be his to keep or sell now, in payment for the burial fee. The undertaker took his gun belt and his ring and other personal effects including his saddle next door to the sheriff's office. No one was there yet, of course, but nonetheless, the old undertaker was honest.

He started right away making the pine casket for six-foot-two Larame Crighton and when it was finished, he laid Larame in it, then positioned it on the side of the street.

For the rest of the day, most all of the townsfolk, at some time or other, came over for a look at the dead outlaw's corpse.

Even Rose, one of the towns "ladies of the night," felt the need to say goodbye to the young cowboy. She had laid with him for two hours just two nights ago.

Rose was special. Yeah, she was a whore like the others, but she was both prettier and more loving than any of the other girls. She loved everyone in town and showed it in her own way. Everyone in town loved her right back. Somehow, she had convinced every stinking one of them that they were her true love, but that they needed to keep it secret. She fucked them long and hard, and poured her love onto them so completely that no one wanted the romance to end, so they kept the secret.

The old, fat, bald undertaker was one of her loves. When Rose showed up to peer into the casket, he ran right out to meet her. She greeted him so politely and smiled at Joe the undertaker with such a vivacious smile that it melted Joe in his boots. He held her hand as she peered down into the casket.

"Oh, my goodness!" she blurted out. "He's trying to say something!"

Now for anyone else, the undertaker would have laughed it off and gone back to work, but Rose was different. If she said he talked, Joe would listen.

They both stared in silence at the corpse, and sure enough both Joe and Rose saw his lips move.

Rose put her ear close to his mouth and was determined to believe that she heard him say, "water."

She rushed to the trough and scooped up some water into her palms and slowly carried it back to Larame.

She saw his tongue peek out as she poured the water onto his lips.

All Joe the undertaker could say was, "Well I'll be damned!"

Larame

Chapter 2

You Stay Dead

Rose stayed by Larame's side late into the night. Every so often she went back to the trough and brought him some drops of water.

Her drowsiness finally overtook her and she returned to the hotel and softly cried into her pillow.

She rushed out at first light to check on her dead friend. She smiled when she realized he had made it through the cold night. This night was tough and rivaled his very first. He wasn't supposed to survive that first night after his birth, and his initial success to life might just be what was allowing him to hang on now.

Rose was sitting by the coffin in a chair that Joe had put out for her, and looked up to see the sheriff and posse returning from the chase.

"You get that god-damned outlaw buried, ya hear, I don't want him stinking up my town!" Sheriff McGraw yelled to Joe the undertaker.

"Sorry, I can't oblige you, Sheriff," Joe answered right back.

"You bury that bastard right now if'in yer wantin to keep yer job!" said the sheriff, now even angrier.

Sheriff McGraw got off his horse and tied it to the rail as all five of his deputies bent over peering into the casket.

"Looks dead to me," one of them said and the others agreed before heading off to the saloon to wash the dust of the trail out of their throats.

Big Jim McGraw walked over to the old fat bald undertaker, looked right down into his eyes, and said, "Bury him! That's an order."

"You ain't got no authority to order me to do anything, Sheriff," Joe spoke holding his ground.

Jim was almost as old as Joe was, but Joe had seen Big Jim handle two young cowboy's half drunk and causing trouble. He cracked them around like peanuts and they left town with a good lesson in their pockets.

Old Joe didn't want any part of that from his longtime friend.

"Sheriff, you know me. If'in I coulda buried this hombre the minute he came in, I woulda, and you know that!" he said, reasoning with the sheriff.

"Well then, why the hell didn't you?" Sheriff McGraw replied.

"Cuz he ain't all the way dead yet," Joe said solemnly.

"That can't be!" the sheriff yelled. "He was stone cold dead two days ago when we found him on the trail! What the hell do you mean he's not all the way dead?"

"Musta come back to life?" Joe said quizzically.

"I can fix that right now!" the sheriff said as he moved closer toward the casket.

At that moment Rose stood up and met him as he approached.

Rose clamped onto his right hand with her left, and cupped his cheek with her right. She looked up and just said, "Jim?"

That pause gave the undertaker time to formulate what he said next.

"This here outlaw was presented to me legally by one of your very own deputies! He is now in my authority to ready him, build a casket, and bury him. No one, not even you, can come between me and that task."

"I'll bury him tomorrow if the good Lord is willing to take him."

"Otherwise, we wait."

Rose turned to Joe and embraced him; she then kissed his shiny bald head.

At some point later that day, Larame felt the drop of cold water hitting his lips, and he managed to slightly open his left blue eye.

He knew that he had finally died. He knew that because he saw the Angel-of-God that was to meet him at heaven's gate.

Now knowing that he had gone to heaven and not to hell, he smiled at his welcoming angel.

Rose saw the faint smile and took it for her own.

Rose rushed to the saloon and enlisted all of the other girls to help her. They borrowed a wheelbarrow and lifted Larame into the tub. They wheeled him right into the saloon and dragged him up the stairwell, placing him inside Rose's room on her bed.

He lay there motionless for three days, with his only action coming when Rose lifted his head for water or warm soup.

His eyes still shut; he took the water and soup without complaint.

Rose then stripped off his still blood-caked clothes and looked at his wound. She took a needle and thread and sewed up the hole in his belly. It was six inches to the right of his navel. Rose didn't know it, but it took out one of his kidneys. She bandaged it and then rolled him over on his side, revealing the massive exit wound.

Rose didn't have any doctoring skill, but she sewed pretty well and sewed his wound and his skin back to where it seemed to need to be. It only bled a small amount, being that he didn't have much blood in him at all.

Patched and bandaged, Rose would spend some time with him each day, lying beside him, coaxing him to both live and heal.

Rose continued her job working at the Morningstar Hotel and Saloon, with the only exception of whoring. Since her bed was taken, she comforted all her suitors with a kiss and convinced them she would be doing the same thing if it was them lying in her bed dying.

They all ended up picking one of the other, less beautiful, girls for their comfort.

The Death and Life of Larame Crighton

Larame

Chapter 3

Here Lies Larame Crighton

The empty casket took on a life of its own. Townsfolk would come around and look inside, noticing the blood-stained bottom. Word was the body was in the hotel. Some figured it to be in number ten, the door on the balcony that always had everyone's attention as it belonged to Rose.

They all liked to speculate on where he was, and on if he was alive or dead.

Sheriff McGraw yelled at the undertaker every day, telling him to do something.

Having enough of the torment, Joe got Lefty, the town drunk, to help him. Together they dragged the empty casket out to the graveyard and dug a shallow grave. They then placed some rocks in the box and lowered it into the ground. It looked from afar like they were saying a prayer before filling it in, but they were actually swearing and wiping their brows from the heat.

"Nobody should have to stand in this god-damned heat and bury a box-a-rocks!" Lefty complained.

"Tell it to the fucking Sheriff!" Joe answered wiping the sweat pouring down the side of his face.

They pounded a marker into the ground at the head of the grave.

Here lies Larame Crighton.

"There, now maybe Big Jim will get the hell off my back!" Joe said aloud.

"Where's my bottle?" Lefty asked.

"I ain't got the fucking thing on me, you know, don't ya?" Joe cried out. But he quickly lamented to his helper. "Sorry, I really thank you for your help, guess the sun's getting to me. I'll buy you a bottle and a top shelf drink when we get back to the saloon, okey-dokey?"

"Sure," Lefty agreed, "long as we go back now!"

When they got back to the saloon, Lefty opted for two cold beers instead of the top shelf whiskey. It wasn't much cooler in the saloon than outside, but there was a gentle breeze that eased the heat.

"Tell you what, Lefty, I'll get you three damn beers if ya want," the undertaker proposed.

"You drive a hard bargain, so I'll accept," Lefty laughed and nodded.

Three beers and a quarter of the way down the bottle, Lefty suddenly stood up and addressed the entire crowd of customers.

"It may say, Here Lies Larame Crighton on the marker out there, but you all should know that he just might burst out of that door, right up there, and we'll all be in a gunfight!"

Lefty looked around and everyone watched as he fell right on his face, unconscious.

One of the patrons took that moment to lash out, "Might as well put Lefty in one of your boxes, Joe. Now or later, don't seem to matter much."

"Mind your manners," Joe replied. "Lefty did a fine job helping me today. I didn't see any of you fellers helping me clean up this town."

Joe dragged Lefty over into a dark corner of the bar and found a clump of rags for him to use as a pillow.

Everything went back to normal, but Lefty was right. Whenever anybody looked up at that door, they got just a little bit edgy.

Larame

Chapter 4

One Scream Leads to Another and Another

The next week saw Rose managing and cooking for the Morningstar Hotel and Saloon. She had taken over almost all the owners' duties, as he went off to Laredo to work out a business deal. Most everyone figured he'd left because he had the heebie-jeebies. He was nervous ever since Rose brought in that cowboy of hers. Nonetheless, the dark dreary place looked a bit more appealing with Rose as its face and business even started to pick up. That is, until later that day.

Rose went in as usual to check on the comatose Larame Crighton. The door shut with a thump and that noise sparked Larame to sit straight up in bed. He looked around and let out a blood-curdling scream. He then fell back down in bed and passed out again.

That scream touched the already jagged nerves of everyone in the whole joint. Some left in a run, and about half of the remaining left in a walk, but either way the place cleared out.

Not one person entered the hotel-saloon, that is, until Sheriff McGraw poked his head in and yelled, "Everything okay in here?"

Rose greeted him at the swinging doors, "Things are just fine, Sheriff, c'mon in."

The big sheriff pushed open the doors, one with each hand. He stepped into the saloon, tall as he could, and studied the room. Not seeing danger, he turned to Rose and asked her what had happened.

Still wary, he listened to Rose give him the details of Larame's meaningless scream. "I just spooked his soul, I figure," she explained.

"I'm gonna have to take a look!" he told her sternly.

"Now you know you can't be doing that, Jim, you have to clear that with the judge when he comes around."

"That's my room right there and you got no right to barge in there, especially with a mean spirit."

"I say everything is fine, and you should agree unless you're fixin' to go back over to the undertaker's office and see who's responsible for that there body."

"C'mon Jim, how 'bout I come over to the sheriff's office after I get everything cleaned up?"

"We could go in one of your cells and pretend that we're locked up together."

Big Jim let out a slight smile and said, "You gonna wear that frilly petticoat I like?"

"Sure, you big oaf," she teased, "and maybe something else special just for you."

They shared a kiss and Sheriff McGraw went on his way, back to his office, with visions of the coming evening dancing in his mind.

That evening turned rowdy and loud as the two lovers, joined at the waist, rolled around in the cell. She screamed almost as loud as the noise from her room, as the sheriff plowed inside her again and again. At one point after a particularly loud scream, she worried that Joe the undertaker would hear her in the attached building next door, and that he might come running to save her. That might be fun too, she thought.

Suddenly, Big Jim picked her up, still deep inside her, and thrust her against the wall. He pinned her helpless with his hips and gave her a proposition.

"Yer gonna help me break outta this here jail, if'in you don't want me to turn you around."

"I'm gonna have to think about that one, Big Jim!" she said seductively.

She quickly decided to play along. "Well, okay, what do I have to do?"

"Okay then, you take off all your clothes, get real naked, ya hear?" he said to her explaining his plan.

"And?" she asked.

"You call the deputy and tell him you got something fer him to look at, whilst you got your back to him."

"When he comes running in, all eyeballing your bare ass, and thinkin' he'll be seeing more, I'll clobber him and we'll make our escape! Got it?"

"I love a good plan," she beamed and proceeded to remove her frilly petticoat and then her bright red panties.

He watched her undress until she was completely naked. "This plan works, and I'll have to have you again, right there up on that sheriff's desk! You be ready for that!"

The plan worked of course, and he did her again and again on that desk, until they both escaped.

She made it back to her room, and he landed on the bed in the back room of his office.

The Death and Life of Larame Crighton

Larame

Chapter 5

Heaven and Hell

The next morning, the sleeping outlaw awoke once again, but this time he just opened his eyes. Slowly he lifted his head up a bit, and that was plenty painful enough to keep him from moving around.

He stared at the beautiful face he saw once again and said aloud, "Is this heaven?"

"No," she answered, "it's Yuma."

"It can't be Yuma!" he whispered. "The law..."

Rose interrupted him, explaining that she had the law under control and that he need not worry about that at all.

"I'll take care of everything," she told him. "You just lie there and heal for now."

She then kissed him on his cheek and he closed his eyes again. His last thought before darkness overtook him again was that he was right, she was an Angel.

The next week saw Larame awake and alert more often. He was eating and drinking a lot more now and had even asked for a beer, but couldn't stomach enough of it to hold any value. She was feeding him three times a day, a bit of soup broth or a small amount of something soft. He was slowly gaining strength. It was really slow.

Also, about that time, Mark Montpelier, the owner of the Morningstar Hotel and Saloon, returned from Laredo.

Mark was crafty and kept the secret of what he was up to. It was Rose that worked it out of him one evening after the place was closed.

Mark had a snootful and started to brag to her. "Now don't you tell anyone, but my plans are to start an assayer office right here in Yuma. Those miners are getting robbed by the prices the assayers are giving them up near the mines. I could offer them a bundle more and still make a killing. I just have to convince them to come down to Yuma for a rest and vacation. You and the girls will make out just fine too! Why, everybody in town would see more business, if those miners find out how much more their gold is worth down here. Money and some fun are just what those guys need."

Rose kept that information tight to her chest and the only one she ever talked to about it was Larame. He was talking more but mostly listening and had even started to sit up to eat. He tried to sit up on the side of the bed, but failed and collapsed sideways on the bed. Rose struggled to right him and they laughed and hugged, happy that he was at least able to try to sit up.

A few days later, he finally made it up to sit on the side of the bed. Rose and Larame sat there talking and telling their tales to each other, her leaving out most of the whoring and him forgetting to mention the thieving.

They laughed and played but his words stopped her dead in her tracks when he started to talk about the future.

"You should buy this place." he spoke.

Rose laughed and just smiled.

"I mean it, for real!" he said again.

"I can't buy this place! I don't have the money to even think about buying this hotel and saloon."

"But you could." he stated.

"How is that?" she asked.

"You go together with the girls and start to save a little each day. You tighten your belts and take better care of your stuff. Sew your clothes before buying new for a while. Eat some beans instead of the fine dining and in a short time you'll have a nice nest egg."

"Not enough to buy this place." Rose commented.

"Well hold on there, maybe it won't be as expensive as you think?" he explained. "I have a plan."

"I just love a good plan!" She squealed, secretly remembering the time in the jail. "So, what is it?"

"Well, if he goes into the assayer's business like you say..." Larame then explained his whole plan. He convinced her that a new assayer would soon come upon a deal that was bigger than he could handle. The profit he would lose if he didn't come up with the money to buy the miners gold would be immense.

He told her that when he needed some cash, all she had to do was make sure that little fucker that shot him at the bank didn't lend him any money! If she could do that, when the time was right, Mr. Montpelier would sell this place for a fraction of its worth, just to finalize his deal. Both you girls and him will get a great deal.

"Rose's Morningstar Hotel and Saloon has a nice ring to it don't it." he said with a smile.

She then hugged him a little bit too hard and she could tell he was trying his best not to grimace.

The traveling judge was due in town the next day and the townsfolk were all giddy with anticipation about what will happen to the outlaw lying low in number ten.

Rose on the other hand bought into the plan hook, line, and sinker. She marched straight across the street and entered the bank foyer. She stood up close to the window so Randy the manager and slimebag that shot Larame could smell her perfume.

"I have some business I need to talk to you about in private." she softly said.

"We're all alone in here." he answered.

"Someone could burst in here at any moment," she blurted, "they'd know everything that we were saying and doing! Be a lamb and open the gate so we can be in real private, okay?"

She smiled, arching her breasts closer to the window. Randy took in a big breath filled with her perfume and silently got up and opened the door. he walked her into the main part of the bank. Rose brushed against him the entire way back to his office.

"What brings you in Rose?" he asked, "What's going on that so private?"

"This isn't a formal meeting, Randy, come sit on the couch with me instead of behind that cold desk."

Randy cocked his head and spied the opening in her bodice showing her cleavage and when she sat down and crossed her legs, he sucked in, a short burst of air.

He approached the couch and she held out her hand to his and motioned for him to sit close beside her.

She could see by the lump in his pants that he was glad she came in.

"Randy, you don't know me very well, but I know you like me and would be upset if someone was doing me wrong. Am I right?"

"Of course, Rose, is it that outlaw?" Randy said with a flair.

"Oh, no, Randy, it's not Larame."

"Then who is this prick that you talk about?"

Rose leaned in and started to cry on Randy's shoulder. "It's none other than my boss, Mark Montpelier."

"Mark?" he exclaimed, "That's hard to believe."

"Yes, it's Mark, Randy. He keeps it well hidden, but in private after work hours he berates me, making me cry. He even raises his hand to me when no one can see."

"Well, I'll march right over there..." he promised, but Rose cut him off.

"No, we can't! He can't know that you know!" Sobbing, she explained that it was her job at stake and that it was something else that he could do to help her.

"What is it?" he asked as she moved her hand onto his thigh.

Promise me you won't ever lend him money, okay? Promise me! Stand up here in front of me and promise with your hand in the air."

Randy stood up and proceeded to make that vow as Rose opened his pants and gave Randy an experience that he had never before had.

Afterward Randy sat down on the couch sweating balls. Hardly able to catch his breath, Rose said, "One more thing."

"Anything," Randy answered taking a big breath.

"You should give Larame one hundred dollars for shooting him."

"What!?" he answered still out of breath.

"Well, you did shoot him and no one wants any payback. A hundred dollars ought to be fair for letting bygones be bygones. Don't you think?"

"Remember, he's going to walk down those stairs wearing his gun belt and spurs one of these days soon, and you would want that to be a time when you're sitting in the saloon all squared up with him, right?"

"Plus, maybe you'd look forward to me coming over here once a week to give you the full story on how things are going, right back here on this couch?"

"Yes, Rose, I'd like that!" Randy answered.

He then got up, opened the safe, and handed her one hundred dollars for Larame, all the while keeping it a secret.

"You promise?" he asked.

She nodded and answered with the same question. "You promise too?" he nodded, and she sashayed right out the door of the bank. *It's my guess that Larame is in heaven,* she thought, as she crossed the street.

Larame

Chapter 6

Tell it to the Judge

First thing the next morning Rose went over to Boots and Saddles. The handsome dark-skinned craftsman was just readying to open his shop when she knocked on the door.

"Be open in just a few!" Terrence White called out from the back room.

You'll open right now if'in you want to start today with a smile.

Hearing Rose's voice, he hurried to the door and let her in, leaving the closed sign still showing.

He ushered her in and smiled as he said, "What brings you over here this fine morn?"

She held out Larame's boots and answered him. "Should be obvious."

"These boots?" He asked.

"No! you silly boy, you must'a heard it by now, it's spreading all over town, I've been a very bad girl!"

Two young boys happened to be walking by the open window and overheard her say that to the bootmaker. They both hunched down, looking around to see if anyone was watching them.

"See, I told you I heard mom say she was a bad girl." One said to the other.

"Shh," said the first.

Inside, Terrence was already rubbing her down, trying to get his hand under her bodice.

"Oh, Terrence don't," she said, and play acted to start to cry. "You're making me naked!"

With that the two boys squinched down even further, getting small as they could and listened with wide eyes.

"You need a spanking, Rose!" he ordered.

The boys heard the bed start squeaking and listened as wap, wap, wap, echoed out the window, "No, no, no, stop, stop, stop," she moaned. The sounds continued getting even louder.

The young'uns were just about to run over to the Sheriff's Office and tell Big Jim when out of nowhere, Rose screamed.

"DON'T STOP, DON'T STOP, HARDER, HARDER!"

Puzzled, the boys took off for school, wondering why anyone would like getting a spanking.

Rose would pick up the boots later that day without saying a word.

Around noon, the Judge rolled in on his carriage. Folks were out en mass to meet him. There wasn't much of a venue. Just a few shopkeeper squabbles and some bills that needed to be addressed.

The main item on the agenda was of course Larame Crighton. That's why Rose sat through all the boring complaints and rulings, waiting for any talk about Larame.

And talk they did!

"What the hell do you mean that he came back to life?" The Judge barked. "A person is either dead or they're not!"

"Judge, we found that outlaw deader than a doornail, lying in the desert sun with his horse nearby."

"Weren't no doubt that he was dead in my eyes or any of my deputies. Simpson hauled him back to Yuma for me. The whole trip back, there wasn't one time that this Larame character was anything but dead! Deputy Simpson will testify to that if you want."

"Go on." ordered the Judge.

Simpson went up to the stand and was sworn in.

"Just like the Sheriff said, he was dead the whole way back." deputy Simpson explained.

"What the hell does "dead the whole way back" mean?" the Judge asked.

"Well, your Honor, it means that he laid across that saddle and didn't move or make any noise at all. Not so much as a peep, the whole way back. See, he couldn't" Simpson testified.

"And why couldn't he?" the Judge scowled, irritated that he even had to ask that question.

"Well, he weren't bleeding. Sashaying around, face down on the back of that horse would'a caused him to bleed out some, but he couldn't. See, he didn't have any blood left in him."

"How are you sure of that?" again the Judge questioned him for clarity.

"Judge, if you saw the ground we raised him up from, you'd know all the man's blood was left there. Everyone was surprised at the amount of clotted blood still stuck to his clothes. If you added it to what lay on the ground there in the desert, well, it was unreal. Nobody has that much blood."

"Is that all, Deputy?"

"No sir!" Simpson answered.

"Well what else do you need to tell the court?" replied the baffled Judge.

Well, I looked that dead outlaw all over, cuz'in he weren't bleeding none and I saw his big artery all shot to pieces. It was sticking right out of his back. If'in there was a drop of blood left in him, it would'a squirted right out at me. Judge, that outlaw was DEAD!

With that information the Judge called a recess for lunch. During the recess Rose approached the Judge to get his take on the information so far.

It quickly became apparent that her charm was just left hanging out there with this Judge. He brushed her off and greeted his good friend Mark Montpelier and they went to his chambers laughing the whole way.

The Judge was in a better mood after lunch. He called the proceeding to order and a young Deputy acting as bailiff, approached the next witness and swore him in.

"Do you, Joe the Undertaker promise to tell the truth, the whole truth, and nothing but the truth, so help you God?"

"I do!" Joe answered.

The Deputy didn't know Joe's last name, it seems that no one else knew it either, so the proceeding continued without a hitch.

"Was this feller dead or not when Deputy Simpson turned him over to you?" asked the Judge, hoping for a quick answer and an end to this hearing.

"He was dead, your Honor."

"Are you sure?" quizzed the Judge.

"He was dead alright, knew it right away, deader than a doornail, he was."

"What's that supposed to mean, explain it to the court?" the Judge continued.

Well, it being a nail, a doornail, is pounded into the wall and bent across the door, done right that door ain't a door at all anymore, no, it just becomes another part of the wall. That outlaw wasn't just dead; he was a corpse.

"I don't make no pine boxes for someone alive, Judge, and I made him a casket that fit him just right. Laid him right out in the street for all to see." Joe concluded.

The Judge then called another recess, but not until he explained that he wanted everyone that saw the dead outlaw lying in the casket in the street, to be present in fifteen minutes. "Go out and tell the others." he said, "anyone wants to say dead or alive can be heard after recess!"

They came back to a full courthouse. The room was overflowing and they left the normally closed double doors open for the people that were spilling over.

Order, order! the Judge cried out.

It took a while, but soon the room was quiet again.

"Alright now," the Judge spoke, "I want any of you that saw the dead man in the casket, to raise your hand if you are sure he was dead!"

Almost everyone in the crowd was waving their arms high in the air, hoping to tell their story to the crowd.

"You all calm down now, we don't need any more testimony to say he was dead.

"I did notice you didn't raise your hand young lady." as he pointed directly at Rose.

"I didn't see a dead man." she replied.

"Bailiff, swear her in right now, I believe her name is Rose." the Judge ordered.

After a quick swearing-in, the Judge bellowed out his question to Rose.

"Are you going to tell this court under oath that all these townsfolk, including the Sheriff and the undertaker, are stone cold liars?"

"Of course not, your Judgeship!" she smiled as she answered.

"Well?" the Judge questioned, "What are you going to tell us you saw?"

"I saw a young man come back to life." she whispered.

She said it low, but the whole courtroom heard her. And a hush came over the already quiet courtroom.

"Back to life?" he asked her again, "you're saying he was dead and come back to life?"

"No!" she barked, "I didn't say that!"

"Well say it again to clear it up for the record." the Judge ordered.

"Everybody else in this courtroom except you and a few others are the ones that saw him dead. When I first looked at him, he started coming back to life. I never saw no dead guy!" Rose repeated.

The Judge called yet another recess.

"I can't make a ruling until I find out if this Larame Crighton is alive or dead. I'll take a few minutes and follow Miss Rose over to the Hotel and see for myself. Everyone can stay right here or follow me over, make up your own mind."

Without exception the entire crowd followed the Judge and Rose, and watched from the tables as they went up the stairs. Hearts stopped when Rose opened the door and let the Judge in, closing the door behind her.

True to plan, Larame lay there as motionless as he could.

The Judge eyed him over and said, "Prove to me he's alive."

Rose offered some water to Larame and he sloppily slurped it up as she held his head.

"That's enough for me," he said returning to the courtroom.

The sheriff had to clear a pathway through the crowd, wondering if the outlaw was indeed dead or alive.

Back in the courtroom, the Judge slammed his gavel and gave his decision.

"If we hang a condemned man, and later cut him down, but he gets back up and walks away, we have to let him go."

"If a man is condemned to death from a firing squad, and none of the bullets hit him, we have to let him go."

"Larame Crighton was not tried or sentenced, because he was dead. His case does not fit under those laws. But his case doesn't fit under any of the other laws either. Therefore, I rule not to make a ruling at this time."

"Larame Crighton does not appear to be a hazardous concern to anyone in this town. My only ruling is that things stay as they are now until I get back next month."

"I will ask my colleagues their opinions and go through the records for a precedent. I know scholars that always proclaim to be smarter than me. This may get interesting."

"I repeat my ruling; everything stays as it is." the judge banged his gavel and closed this session of court.

The Death and Life of Larame Crighton

Larame

Chapter 7

Ducks All Lined Up in a Row

Everything was looking up for both Rose and Larame. With the Judge's order in place, Rose had at least a month to put everything in order. Every day, she would have to play out a piece of the puzzle that would make Larame Crighton a free man.

Rose slipped over to the mercantile at the edge of town, right after the dinner crowd. She had made bowls of soup and some plates of beans and laid them out, for any customers that straggled in late.

The Country Mercantile was busy this early evening, and Matt was dashing all around helping customers.

When he finally got to Rose, he stopped and took in a big breath.

"Fine to see you, Rose" he said with a sly smile.

"Fine to see you too, Matt." she purred.

"What brings you in today?" he asked biting his lip.

"Oh well, this and that, you know me, always searching a good deal." she said, while reaching down his pants with her right hand.

Matt quickly turned towards the table where the good shirts were displayed to hide Roses actions.

They angled in close together as she fingered a sharp new shirt that would fit Larame perfectly.

"Don't suppose there's a good deal to be had with this shirt, is there?" she said softly in his ear, all the while stroking Matt real slow so as not to create a scene.

"Seems like your wantin me to just give it to you for free." Matt whispered back.

Rose handed him the shirt and in one smooth swoop, she reached in her bra and took out a small silk handkerchief, and pushed her other hand down into his pants joining the first.

"Rose," Matt panted, "people will see!"

"Let'em see if they want" she said as she squirted him into her silky-smooth kerchief. She then bunched it up and pulled out her hands, carefully replacing the handkerchief back into her brassiere.

"I'll keep this close to me," she said with a wicked smile, "I might need it again later tonight."

Matt smiled and said, "I sure hope so," as he wrapped up the shirt for her.

Rose blew him a kiss as she left the store.

She returned to her duties and the place was busy. The girls were out in their finest and men were huddled around them laughing and grinning.

"What's causing all the special attention tonight?" Rose asked her friend Dolly.

Dolly explained what had transpired, quietly as she could.

"Seems we were all up there in number nine, right next to your room, havin a bath cuz they just brought up clean hot water. Well, umm, anyway, we started one by one taking a bath and helping each other scrub, to speed things up, wantin our turn before the water got cold."

"Guess we got kinda loud and having some special fun whilst the menfolk were down here listening. Our playing around got sorta more serious and to mock us, Lola opened the door just a little, and started to moan."

"Oh! Oh! OH!" Lola moaned, her mouth in the crack of the door.

All the men staring at the balcony wanted more than anything else to peek in there to see the show, but they all knew that if they did, they would be kicked out for sure, and none were willing to risk that fate.

Dolly continued her story, "Soon as someone finished bathing, while we were still laughing and scrubbing, they went out the door running down the balcony, back to their room. Seems that was in full view, and we were covering up with only a towel for our modesty."

"When Lola went running, she dropped her towel and had to run back to get it, all to the applause and hooting from all the guys in the saloon."

"I guess they got horny?" Dolly finished.

"Well, that worked out just fine now, didn't it?" Rose quietly said to her, "Go along, you join the fun!"

Rose sat back and watched how the men were reacting and made a note to have hot water delivered to room number nine, every Friday around ten o'clock, well after the families had finished dinner and went back home.

The next morning, Rose visited Clint at the county records office. Clint was just a clerk there, but he was almost always alone, as there weren't many duties to perform.

Seeing Rose, like every other man in town, he was both surprised and happy to see her come in.

Rose leaned against the high counter, her firm breasts lying all by themselves, flat on the countertop.

"You need to show me something right away," she said, in her sexiest voice.

Clint paused taking in the sight and thought to himself, *you need to show me something really quick too!* But instead, all he said was, "Hi Rose, what can I help you with?"

"Open the gate so I can get around back there with you, we have to look up something and I don't remember all the details."

Clint's boss hadn't been around in weeks so he looked around and reluctantly allowed Rose back into the storehouse.

Boxes and boxes were stacked, marked mostly by their date, but some by their importance like the time the fire almost destroyed the town.

Rose saw that box that said "FIRE" and wished there was one for a lost boy.

"Find me a record for a Buster something or other that got lost maybe ten or so years ago."

"Gee, Rose, that ain't much to go on." he said as she moved closer to him.

"I think his last name started with a "C." she added.

They were sitting on a hard bench in the back and he had a big box on his lap.

Rose didn't have a chance to charm young Clint as he always had a box on his lap and couldn't stop talking about his young sweetheart that he was planning to marry someday.

"What about this?" he asked as he was looking in the sixth or seventh box of records.

"Let's, see?" Rose asked, as he handed her a worn poster.

The poster showed a big hand drawing of a handsome young man, maybe around fourteen or fifteen. There were big letters saying "Anyone seen this boy?"

It wasn't much, but Clint promised to keep searching for more information about that poster, as Rose kissed him on the cheek and went back to her hotel.

It's a start, she thought as she fed, then lay, beside Larame for a while before having to start the lunch menu.

All the girls were helping with the place more than usual and they were more than generous at putting some money in the kitty for their future. They were always making the place nicer knowing they didn't have to, but seeing a new day coming and hoping they were to be the owners someday.

The girls took to sewing more and even started sharing their clothes so that everyone had something different to wear without having to buy new. Plus, the idea of owning the whole place, eliminated the petty fighting over clients, as now it didn't matter who turned the trick, as long as the extra money got put into the savings pile.

So far it was a good month for Rose and the girls.

Rose still had things to handle. She went to the Sheriff's office to see about getting Larame's personal effects but he wasn't there, so she headed towards the livery to check on Star and see about getting him back. On the way the barrel maker stepped out his front door and waved to Rose.

"Fine morning, Rose," he shouted, "you need a barrel you come see me, okay?"

Rose wheeled around and marched right up to him.

"I sure will Henry!" she teased. She pushed up towards him and said, "you know you sure are a handsome man," as she caressed the front of his pants.

"Step inside," he pleaded, and she did. Rose emerged an hour later to resume her task.

Henry stood in his doorway again, wiping the sweat from his brow and watching her walk all the way down the street until she disappeared into the stable.

Once inside the stable, Rose found Lefty still passed out, lying in a pile of hay just outside Star's stall. She then sat down beside him and pulled the top of her dress and her brassiere off her shoulder exposing her breast. She snuggled up beside the sleeping drunk and positioned herself so that he was suckling her perfect teat.

She poked Lefty in the ribs and startled, he woke up. Sucking her breast, he stopped long enough to ask her if he was in heaven.

"No Lefty, this is Yuma," she told him chuckling to a private joke. "Not only that, we're in a stable that stinks to high hell! Add to that that we're lying in hay half mixed with horseshit, and well, no, it ain't heaven at all."

"It's fine enough by me." he told her still suckling, while reaching inside her dress for her other breast.

"You like me taking good care of you now, don't you, Lefty?" she said with a smile.

"Sure do!" he mumbled barely stopping to talk.

"I want you to be doing something for me, is that a deal, Lefty?"

"Anything you say, Rose!" he now shifted to holding both her breasts, one with each hand, squeezing them and rubbing her nipples.

"I want you to take special care of Star for me, you hear?" she explained as he took to sucking one nipple then the other.

"You mean Joe's horse?" he asked still playing with her silky-smooth bosom.

"Might not be Joe's for long, but don't worry about that, just take good care of him, for me, okay?"

"Sure Rose." he agreed.

She pulled away and then leaned in to Lefty rubbing her breasts back and forth against his face. She then sat up and put her charms away, reminding Lefty that if he wanted to play around ever again, Star better be well groomed.

She walked back to the Hotel hoping no one would approach her. The smell on her dress wasn't going to be easy to get off.

Larame

Chapter 8

Buddy Collins

Over the next few days, Rose teased out a new hat, belt, and some britches from the hatter and the shopkeepers. Everyone loved Rose's visits, even if it meant that it would cost them something or other.

His new outfit just needed one more thing to make her happy. She needed him to have some silk underdrawers and a silk undershirt.

She figured white silk would be good, and since she would be the only one seeing them, she imagined some small red hearts all over them. She was getting hot just thinking about him lying there in her bed wearing the new undies.

She marched over to the local seamstress and told her the design.

Grace looked up at her from her chair at the sewing machine and gave her a wicked smile.

"Get that thought out of your head right now, Grace!" Rose exclaimed. "You won't be seeing that image anytime soon."

"What about me getting a little bit carved off the price?" she asked the young seamstress. "Anything I can do to make it easier for you?"

The young, naive girl didn't catch on at all. Instead, she said, "Yes, my feet are sore, and you could press the treadle back and forth for me as I sew."

Rose sat quietly and watched as the very pretty girl cut the silk material into the patterns of the white and heart undergarments; she was getting ready to sew.

Rose sat across from Grace at the sewing machine and pedaled to make the whole undershirt.

"That looks perfect!" Rose exclaimed.

"It feels very nice as well," Grace answered.

"I just have to see it on," Rose pleaded. "Try it on so I can see it, okay?"

"Geez, Rose, it's too big for me."

"It'll be fine," Rose said as she approached Grace and lifted off her grungy work shirt in one swift motion. Grace balked when Rose unclasped her bra.

"You'll want to feel the material on your beautiful breasts," she spoke as she tried to convince her.

"Oh, okay, I guess," and she proceeded to let Rose remove all her clothes.

Completely naked, Rose helped her put on the oversized shirt. It went all the way down to her knees, and Grace twirled around, feeling the silky softness all over her body.

"We're done; I'll stay and help you make one of these shirts for yourself," Rose offered the young, pretty Grace. "If you come over to my place later tonight wearing this shirt, all the men will be clambering around you."

Grace twirled around again, feeling herself up and down her body with her hands, loving the soft, silky feeling the shirt gave her.

Rose hugged her from behind and whispered in her ear, "Back to work," is all she said, as she guided Grace back into her chair.

"But you must be tired of pedaling, aren't your feet sore?" Grace reasoned.

"Yes, they are, so I'll try something a little different now," Rose answered.

She found a throw pillow on the couch and positioned it on the floor under the machine and proceeded to kneel on it. She then started to move the treadle back and forth with her hands.

Rose couldn't help watching Grace's cute little flower twitching under that silk shirt.

It was when Grace said, "Last piece," and sewed for a bit, then stopped when Rose pushed forward, burying her face between Grace's legs.

Grace instantly arched and took a big breath. Still fantasizing about all the men looking at her at the saloon, she relaxed and closed her eyes.

It wasn't long, as the feeling inside her grew stronger and stronger, that Grace's young body exploded, and she clutched her own breasts as spasm after spasm left her, leaving her body limp.

She relaxed her thighs that had been squeezing Rose's head and sat there in ecstasy. She wanted to kiss Rose for giving her this new experience, but Rose wasn't done.

Once again, Rose stuck out her tongue and pushed her face into Grace's damp lap.

Grace squealed and leaned way back, allowing the magic to take over her body. She pinched her nipples real hard as the feeling once again rose up in her loins. It didn't take long, and soon she was writhing and squirming all over her chair as she clamped on to Rose's face and head.

Her orgasms continued, one after another, jerking her whole body every time.

When it was finally over, she sat there, still leaning back, sprawled in her chair. Her hair was disheveled, and the new shirt was wide open, exposing her large breasts.

The position and exposure didn't bother Grace one bit anymore.

Grace took off the shirt and folded it neatly. She then took the short silky pants and folded them too. She put them together and wrapped them in brown paper.

As she held them out to Rose, still naked, Rose gave her a deep kiss and reminded her that she would come over and help her make a shirt for herself, and this time, Grace got the message, smiled, and said, "I'd love that!"

Rose couldn't wait much longer before she lay her naked body atop Larame as he wore the very pajamas she was carrying home. She fantasized about that the whole walk back to the hotel.

Rose returned to find Larame, fully dressed, sitting in a chair, and Lola standing right beside him.

Lola started talking before Rose got a thought out.

"I heard a crash and came running, your room being right next to mine and all. Found your manfriend on the floor trying to get back up. I just finished helping him when you burst in."

Larame smiled at her as Lola scurried out.

"That's okay, Lola," she yelled to the closing door.

"Look at you all fancy dressed up, planning on going somewhere?" Rose said as she caressed his cheek and gave him a kiss.

"I'm fixin' on coming down those stairs and pulling some of my own weight around here tonight. I hear Friday night's a real scorcher around here, and I figure I'd rather be a part of it than lying here listening."

"You make it down those stairs by yourself, and I'll be more than happy to find you something to do." She then kissed him again and raced back down to the kitchen to make all the food for the crowd that was starting to shuffle in.

It was a bigger-than-normal crowd as some of the men, expecting a show, came in early to get a good seat.

The families were all off on the edges, as normal, but Rose spied three of the new church ladies sitting at a table in the darkest corner.

To their spite, Rose took their order herself and welcomed them to the Morningstar Hotel and Saloon.

They ordered the fish dinner, and Rose was glad, as one of the men had brought her three big catfish that she was going to have to cook up tonight whether anyone wanted them or not.

She sashayed back to the kitchen, and one of the church ladies said, "She looks like a whore to me." The next said, "She smells like a whore, that's for sure." "She even walks like a whore," commented the last.

Later, they all said they hated the meal and left in a huff, leaving perfectly cleaned plates from the three huge catfish.

Rose looked around and was just about to give the signal to the girls to start the show when the door marked number ten came wide open. You could have heard a pin drop as Larame Crighton walked out of that room and approached the balcony.

With both hands on the railing, he stretched to see all the folks looking up at him.

"Howdy, folks," was the best he could muster.

He walked down the balcony and stopped at room number nine, peered in, then tipped his hat, closing the door. He didn't know that it was left a little bit open on purpose for the coming show.

He turned and slowly started descending the long staircase.

One step, then two, then three, but on the fourth step down, his knee and strength gave way. He barely caught himself as he held on to the railing and sat on the fifth step down.

Quickly, he pulled himself back up, seeing that everyone was watching him now that the bath door was closed.

He took two more stairs before falling again and reluctantly came down the rest on his backside, not wanting to risk going head over heels.

Once at the bottom, Rose helped him up onto a chair. She then knelt down beside him, pulling off his boots. She replaced them with some slippers that Matt from the Mercantile brought over, hoping for some favor.

She then placed an apron over his neck, tied it in the back, and handed him her bar cloth.

Larame started slowly but moved the bar-rag back and forth across the table, cleaning half the table spotless.

He worked his way to the other side of the table, holding on to the chairs, and plopped down on the opposite side chair, wiping the other half of the table clean too.

Larame was cleaning tables when Rose finally gave the signal to start the show.

One by one, the six girls slowly crossed the balcony and disappeared into room number nine. Each one was dressed only in their sexiest underwear, garters, and stockings. They crossed the runway high above the watching crowd, and to each of their delight, heard a round of applause and catcalls.

After a pause to let the men cool off a bit, the girls emerged in a line, one following the next, and came down the stairs, each posing and bending over to show their backsides, and all six carrying a bucket.

They danced right through the middle of the crowd in single file and went straight out the swinging doors. Some of the men tried to get a feel of the girls' bottoms, but were quickly slapped down or bonked in the head with an empty bucket.

"Them's my buckets," Henry proudly shouted out, surrounded by the crowd, "Made 'em this morn!"

A few minutes later, the ladies reappeared in the doorway, each carrying a full bucket of steaming hot water. This time, the crowd parted, giving them plenty of room. Everyone listened as they poured the hot water into the tub, laughing and giggling as they played with each other.

One of the girls yelled, "Someone's pushing on my bottom with their hip while I'm trying to pour out my water!" The crowd howled when they heard another girl call out, "That weren't my hip!"

The men were being worked up to a frenzy when the girls went back outside for another round of hot water.

It was while they waited for their return that Clint from the records department ran into the saloon and yelled at the top of his lungs, "BUDDY COLLINS! I found him, Rose. I found Buddy Collins. Buddy went missing years ago, but it's all right here in this piece of a newspaper I found in the records."

Clint held the paper up, surprised that no one in the crowd was interested in his discovery, but Rose ran right over to him; she was interested in the news.

Larame's life and death could very well be hanging on this old newspaper clipping.

"He's right over there," Rose said, pointing at Larame wiping off a table while the customers stood nearby, waiting for him to finish.

True to plan, Clint ran right over to Buddy and, in the middle of the biggest crowd in the Morningstar Hotel and Saloon's history, shook his hand and yelled, "Hi, Buddy! Glad to meet you, glad you finally made it back home!"

He then stepped back and yelled out again, "Hey, everybody! It's Buddy, Buddy Collins, he ain't lost no more! Buddy made it back home to Yuma!"

He then went over to Rose, where she hugged and kissed him again and again on the cheek.

Larame

Chapter 9

The Show's a-Just Start'in

The girls continued to take the buckets of hot water up to room number nine, when one of the men in the crowd, yelled out, "She changed her britches! Look, she's wearing the same yellow panties that dark-haired girl had on!"

Another guy in the crowd piped up louder than the others, "They've been getting naked up there every on every trip, I noticed that myself!"

The girls all blushed as they went up the stairs and announced that they now had enough water for their bath.

Leaving the door almost halfway open this time, they splashed and washed each other in the tub of hot water. Over and over the girls would push each other towards the spot where the gawkers could see.

The sounds got louder and louder up there, and the splashing and squealing, the ooohs and ahhhs, sounded more and more like a sex party than a bath.

Dolly was the first one done with her bath. She was already hot and bothered from all of the girls rubbing all over her body, getting every part of her nice and clean.

She stepped out of the room number nine, and trotted towards her room, holding a towel around her waist. Suddenly she stopped and turned to the crowd that was cheering her on, and flashed open the towel, for just one second, before continuing back to her room.

One after another the girls dashed to their rooms, either half naked or naked, sometimes stopping for a second and twirling around, giving the boys a big eyeful.

Rose was so busy she couldn't carry the beer to the tables fast enough. Buddy was now behind the bar filling glasses with beer, as quickly as he could. He happily missed most of the show.

Lola was the last one done with her bath. "Are you boys ready?" she yelled from inside the room.

The whole crowd started to chant, Lola, Lola, Lola! And she appeared naked but for a towel around her waist and cupping her huge breasts with her hands. A bit of murmur started as the crowd expected something a bit more, but that turned to ohhs, and ahhs as she raised her hands into the air, started running and did two cartwheels, one right after another, ending up standing legs spread and arms straight up in the air. She yelled TAA DAAA! before disappearing into the shadows at the end of the balcony.

The crowd went wild.

Almost as much beer was spilled after that move, then was drunk, as everyone was elbowing and nudging the guys all around them crying out, "Did you see that?"

It took a while before the girls were ready and came back downstairs, but they were dressed to the nines, and not one person left because of the wait.

Wave after wave of men went up those stairs, their arms draped with a girl, only to get marched back down those same stairs, a few minutes later, with a half-naked girl at their side. The girls would quickly run up to room nine, and jump in that tub, scrub up good, then call up the next suitor.

This went on for hours until the last man left with a smile on his face.

Larame

Chapter 10

Save the Safe

The new assayer's building was going up fast. It was located strategically straight across the street from the sheriff's office. There were two big windows in the front, so anyone inside could see a good bit of the town outside, but right smack in the middle of their view would be the big sign that read "SHERIFF'S OFFICE."

That sign would go a long way to help customers know the safety of their gold.

The safe he was having delivered would finish that same job.

Buddy had taken to hanging around watching the work and the frame of the building go up, when Mark Montpelier offered him a job with the construction. Buddy agreed and started helping out wherever he could. He couldn't do much, but everyone was willing to help him anytime he started to struggle. Buddy was well liked by the other workers, and Mark realized his value even if it was just keeping morale up high.

The next day, work came to a standstill as they had finished preparations for the safe, and were notified that it was on its way, just outside of town.

A crowd had gathered as they could see the enormous safe slowly approaching on the trail.

The safe, sitting on top of a thick, sturdy flat-bed wagon, pulled by sixteen big

Clydesdale horses, pulled into town in full view of all the gawkers.

Mark ran out to meet the old-grizzled driver. They put their heads together and talked a bit, but soon the old-timer got pissed and started screaming at Mr. Montpelier.

"I'm just to deliver this here safe to you, I ain't got nothing to do with the unloading of it," the driver yelled and complained.

"I did my job; now you do yours and get this damn safe off my wagon."

Mark looked around and realized that he didn't have anywhere near enough men to even budge that safe one inch. The crowd, filled mostly with small boys and womenfolk, wasn't going to be any help either.

Mark turned to his workers and asked, "Anyone got an idea of how the hell we're going to get that safe off this wagon and put it back where it belongs?"

There was a murmur between them as they all put their heads together, and finally the foreman approached Mark and told him, "No! It's too big and heavy for us to drag off that wagon."

Mark shook his head, unwilling to be stopped by a problem like this. He looked at the old driver and then turned to his men again.

Let me rephrase that question to you all again: "Does anyone of you men have any, crazy as they may be, ideas about this here safe and getting it to its final resting place?"

Mark Montpelier stood there in front of all his workers as they shook their heads no.

Still, Mark waited, motioning the delivery driver to just wait, too.

In the back of all the men, Buddy was sitting down to rest, but he raised his hand as if he were in school.

"Yes, Buddy?" Mark asked.

"Well, if you really want a crazy answer to what you should do, I just might have one for you," Buddy explained.

Mark approached Buddy and put his hand on Buddy's shoulder and they leaned in to each other, talking quietly as they walked into the shell of the building.

The framework was complete, but no boards were put up, so they walked through the walls like they weren't even there and continued to the back of the building.

Buddy was pointing, then so was Mark, at some of the boards back there, and they talked for a good bit before Mark came back out front and smiled at the driver.

He called over his foreman and told him to go to the stable and get his fine buckboard.

"Just go get it; you'll see when you get back," Mark barked.

The old driver, chewing tobacco, spit a big ugly wad on the ground, and asked Mark what he planned.

"Wait another second, I've put together a plan for the safe," he told the grizzled old man.

Shortly, the foreman emerged from the stable, driving the shiny surrey-topped buggy. It was the nicest buckboard in town and it drew a lot of attention whenever Mark brought it out or returned from a trip.

"How about I trade you this new fine shiny buckboard for that broken-down old flat-bed wagon? Is that a deal you could make?"

The old man's eyes lit up and said, "You mean to trade that buggy for this old wagon?"

"That's my offer," Mark replied.

"Well, start unbuckling my team, cuz I'll make that trade in a heartbeat," he quickly answered.

"Not so fast," Mark yelled, "first you have to position the wagon in the right place, then we'll unfasten the horses."

"No problem," he answered, "where do you want the wagon dropped off?"

Mark Montpelier climbed up onto the wagon next to the old driver and they talked for a while, waving their hands and pointing at the partially built structure. Soon enough they shook hands and Mark got off just as the old driver whipped up the team and slowly proceeded back out of town with the safe.

Everyone looking on was really puzzled, but remembered that this was indeed a crazy plan.

Mark and Buddy led the foreman and some workers out back of the building and started to point at some of the timber already nailed in place. The workers started to remove some of the pieces with a sledgehammer and others started to install braces to strengthen the now-weakened structure.

It was about that time that the flat-bed wagon, drawn by those sixteen horses, made a sharp turn to the right, off the trail it came in on, and into the field.

They saw that same team show up again, back out in the field behind the new assayer's building. Still puzzled, they watched the Clydesdales turn once again, now heading back straight towards them. Those big horses balked, but slowly entered the hole the workers had just made for them.

They pulled the wagon right into the building and stopped.

"A few inches more!" Buddy yelled up to Mark. And the safe inched forward. "A bit more!?" he called out, and the old wagon creaked ahead and stopped abruptly when he heard the words, "Good! That's good right there!"

"Unhitch those Clydesdales!" Mark ordered, and the crowd moved in closer, wondering what his next move was going to be. How's he going to get that wagon out of there, and not the safe? They all wondered.

They released those horses from their heavy load and proceeded to hitch them all up to that tiny, shiny, brand-new buckboard.

It looked funny as hell as all those great big horses pulled out of town hauling that pretty little carriage behind it.

The old guy was missing a front tooth, and that fact showed up clear as he smiled from ear to ear as he left town.

What happened next turned out to be the crazy part of this situation. Armed with some axes, the workers just started chopping at the wagon's wheels. As soon as the first wheel broke down, that corner of the wagon dropped down with a thud. Wheel after wheel broke until the bed of the wagon was flush on the ground.

"That wagon ain't never gonna come outta that there building!" Joe the undertaker yelled, as he had become one of the onlookers.

The workers chopped at the remaining parts of the wheels and trimmed off the axles, making it a fitting support for the huge, heavy safe.

"Hooray!" one of the workers shouted, and they all headed down to the Morningstar Saloon to celebrate.

Mark Montpelier was happy! Buddy was happy, and Rose was happy when she saw the whole town coming her way, hooting and hollering.

Larame

Chapter 11

Star

The next day, Rose moseyed over to the Sheriff's Office to try to argue the Sheriff into giving up Larame's possessions and handing them all over to Buddy. She worked hard on her speech to convince him, but didn't need most of it because the Sheriff agreed without much of a fight.

"Belongs to a dead guy! Far as I'm concerned. If you and Buddy want it, you take it, been cluttering up my space here for long enough. I have to step over that damn saddle every time I reach for my rifle."

Rose scooped up the smaller items on his desk and slung the holster with Larame's Colt forty-five over her shoulder, winked at Big Jim, and headed back to her room. On the way there she passed Boots and Saddles and Terrence, just happened to see her out on the street.

"Morning, Rose!" Terrence called out as she passed.

Rose stopped and wheeled around in her tracks. "Just the person I wanted to see, you big hunk!"

Terrence looked around to see if anyone heard, and said, "Rose, hold your tongue." He continued, "Least anyone hears you and gets the wrong impression."

"You mean the right impression now, Terrence."

"Come in, come in, no need to share my business with the whole town," he pleaded.

"Those new church ladies got to you already, am I right?" she asked.

"They seem to be right-fine people and are bringing me a handsome amount of business!"

"Well then, that sure is good for this town. I hear two more new families are moving in." She relented.

"What can I do for you?" he asked, right out.

"Thought you'd never ask, you-being all interested in church ladies and all. I need you to go over to the Sheriff's and drag that saddle over here and clean it up. It's pretty blood-stained, but it's a good-quality saddle under the blood and trail dirt. You willing to clean up this rig over my shoulder?"

"Sure, Rose, but it will take a long time after I'm done for you to come pick it up."

"No, you need to carry the saddle over to the livery when it's ready, and bring the holster and gun to the Saloon. Be sure to wrap it in paper so the church ladies don't be knowing our business either."

"And my pay?" he asked.

"Well, Terrence, ain't knowing the fact that you'll end up smiling, enough pay to get you started on this?" she scolded.

"Sorry, Ma'am," he said, lowering his head.

Terrence watched Rose, walk all the way to the Saloon. He sure loved to see her walking away.

Rose figured she'd have to figure out what to do about Star tomorrow. The Judge was due back in town in two days and she didn't want to have any loose ends to tie up after he made his verdict.

Guilty or innocent, she wanted Buddy Collins to have all Larame Crighton's possessions. If necessary, he would have to leave town in a hurry, never to return. That was a terrible, sad thought to Rose, but she didn't bring him back to life only to see him hung by the neck.

Rose ran into another church lady later that day. This time there was a group of four of them. They pointed out some stakes that were hammered into the ground and explained that it was where the new church was going to be built. Rose wasn't too happy about a church right across from her Saloon, but she didn't have the same misgivings about it as the church ladies, who were the ones objecting to the Saloon.

Never minding that the Saloon was there long before the church, those damn ladies figured they could push the Saloon right out of town.

"Maybe you could just take down the big sign and put up a little one by the door?" they asked in the politest manner they could muster.

"Maybe I could do just that!" she answered. "Everybody already knows my place is a hotel and Saloon."

"Are you fixing to have a steeple on that church?" she asked.

"Of course!" they answered in unison.

"And a bell, too?" Rose asked.

"Yes, we will have a large bell in the steeple of our new church. Why do you ask?"

"Because if you have a steeple and a bell, everyone will know that it's a church and you won't need a sign either!"

"You don't put up a church sign, and I'll take down my sign, is that a deal?" Rose held out her hand to shake, but the church ladies just turned away, muttering, "Well, I'll be!"

Rose continued over to the stable. Lefty, still a bit drunk from the night before, was doing his best to brush Star. Star liked Lefty in an odd kind of way; it was like he knew that even if Lefty got cantankerous, he was still harmless. Lefty put down the brush and hugged Star, then sweetly greeted Rose.

"Been on my mind all morn!" he said, as charming as a dirty old drunk could tease. "How 'bout a sniff of the twins?" he begged, opening the stall and showing her how handsome the horse looked.

"You're doing a good job with that horse, Lefty, so come here and I'll give you some lovin'." She opened the shirt and his dirty face mashed into her bare chest.

She let him play around for a while, as he slobbered, licked, and kissed her glorious chest and charms.

"I want you to have Star all saddled and ready tomorrow. Can you do that?" Rose asked.

"You clear that with Joe?" he mumbled.

"You let me handle Joe, Lefty, just get Star all ready and have him tied to the rail outside the Saloon before the Judge gets to town."

"Sure," he answered.

"Not just 'sure,' Lefty. You do that right, or the closest thing to my perfume, you'll be smellin', will be that horseshit you've been laying in."

"You got it, Rose; he'll be standing there first thing in the morning, all brushed and ready. I'll make damn sure Star looks clean and stout."

Lefty was well past doing anything more with Rose than he had just done. The rotgut he drank had fouled up his innards so completely that his manhood had vanished years ago.

He did like playing with the prettiest girl in town's titties, and that gave him cause to go on.

Rose moved on to meet up with Joe. She burst into the undertaker's office and caught him reading the paper at his desk, wearing only his underwear.

"Rose, excuse me, I wasn't expecting anyone," he said, and he got up and rushed back into his room to get some clothes.

Rose followed him on his heels and yelled at him when he reached for some pants. "You leave those britches right where they be now, ya hear?"

Joe froze in his tracks and looked back at her as she ordered him to lie down on the bed.

He lay down, but she barked, "On yer back!" So, he rolled onto his back in near panic.

When she grabbed some rope and started tying his leg to the bed, the panic left and he gave a slight smile. Joe knew this game.

Rose yanked his other leg and tied it tight while saying, "We got something important to tend to."

Joe asked her what this was all about as she tied his hands to their respective bedposts.

"It's about Star!" she answered.

The conversation ended right there, as she hoisted her frilly dress up over her head, exposing her bright-red panties. Joe was panting as he watched her slowly pull them down to her ankles. She stood there a bit to give him a good look before dropping the dress and kicking the panties the rest of the way off.

Joe liked this game better than any of the other stuff they played out, and Rose knew it.

Rose bent over and picked them up, bringing them to her nose as she drew a big breath. She then reached out and held them to Joe's nose, pushing them into his face. Joe's erection grew larger than normal as she balled the panties up and stuffed them into Joe's drooling mouth.

She opened the little drawer on his nightstand, and just where she last put it was a little black ball with a loop at each side. She positioned the contraption in Joe's mouth and stretched the loops onto each of his ears. His muffled cries didn't mean anything to her now, as he could hardly produce any sound at all.

"You going to answer my questions?" she ordered.

Joe was squirming and shaking his head "yes."

"Wait here!" she demanded, and left the room, closing the door behind her.

Joe froze. *"Don't leave me here like this,"* he thought.

Soon the door opened again, and to his relief it was Rose, and only Rose.

The tension rose as she approached the bed, now holding his buggy whip, which was in the corner of his office by the door.

Rose was slapping the whip into her palm and demanding he tell the truth.

He was shaking his head "yes" as fast as he could when she blurted out her question. "Did you and Lefty bury Larame Crighton out there behind the old church?"

"Yes," he nodded.

"Liar!" she screamed, almost loud enough for the Sheriff next door to hear.

"Snap," she smacked him on his bare belly with the whip.

"Did you bury Larame out there or not?" she demanded.

Not knowing whether to shake his head "yes" or "no," Joe just lay there.

"Answer me!" she demanded again.

And, "Snap!" she whipped him right across the right nipple.

Wincing in pain, he chose "no," and was shaking his head back and forth.

"You're right!" she said, as, "Snap!" she whipped his left nipple to match.

Joe screamed, but the only sound was a muffled whimper.

"You kept that horse like you completed the job, but you didn't, did you?" she said as she held the whip out, ready to strike.

He shook his head rapidly back and forth, meaning "no."

Rose saw him start to get excited and start to rise. "Snap!" he whimpered and went instantly soft.

Rose climbed onto the bed; Joe was ready to be done with the game, but as she stood up on the bed, he realized she had other plans.

She positioned herself standing on the foot of the bed between his legs, trying to keep her balance. She then slowly lifted her dress, showing him her jewel. Glad he was only gagged and not blindfolded; his member rose again.

Rose dropped her dress and positioned the toe of her foot on his ball sack. As she pressed down on his nut, she asked Joe, "Have you been a bad boy?"

He shook his head "yes," as he grimaced in pain.

"You going to give Star to Buddy?" she asked, pressing down on the nut even more.

"Yes," his head nodded again.

"That's good, to make up for what you done bad, Joe," she spouted as she ground down on his ball, back and forth, like she was putting out a cigar on the street.

Joe's body was lost in pain; he was about to black out when she let up. Pain rang back and forth in his body when, once again, she lifted her dress.

As hurt as he was, seeing her body through his blurry eyes, his body revolted against the pain and his mast came to attention.

The pain from his balls was just subsiding as she slowly lowered herself onto him.

She rose and settled; over and over, and on just the sixth time down, he exploded inside her.

She got off the bed and stood beside him and removed the gag. He held his mouth closed as she attempted to retrieve her panties. Instead, she untied his hands but left his feet to him to untie, as she bent down and kissed his bald head.

She smiled at him and said goodbye, and he smiled back as best he could with that mouthful. She wouldn't be getting those red panties back; no, they were to be nailed onto the wall just above his bed. He wanted them in plain view for Sheriff McGraw. If he ever sees in here and wonders if they're the same ones, he was bragging about Rose wearing special ones for him one night; only Joe would know the answer for sure.

She walked back to the Morningstar Hotel and Saloon, feeling the cool air rise up under her dress. It felt nice. The wind blew at her dress the whole way, and, try as she might, she could only manage to keep the front of her dress held down. The back of her dress went up and down much to the wind's desire. It was held up good and long on one particular burst of wind, and the two boys that heard her before got a nice long view of her bare bottom.

"She ain't wearing no knickers," the older one giggled.

"She's got red marks from a spanking!" the other said, but it must have been his imagination, as her ass was smooth and white as snow.

They scurried home, and their mom was surprised as they both wanted to go to bed early that evening.

The Death and Life of Larame Crighton

Larame

Chapter 12

Here Comes the Judge

The next morning, Star was there on the rail all right, looking healthy and strong.

The Judge arrived right on schedule and quickly disappeared with his old friend Mark.

On the agenda today was a whole mess o' things, as Big Jim would say. There was the okaying of the buildings, both the Assayer's office and the new church, but also the new houses being built on the hill, specifically for the new church people coming to town. Yuma didn't have a mayor, and the papers the Judge would sign didn't hold much weight, as if that's what and where they wanted to build the town, the Judge didn't care much at all. It was Clint, covering for his missing boss, that wanted things nice and legal so he wouldn't get in any trouble when his boss showed back up again.

The Judge signed all those papers right away after bringing the session to order. Rose sat through every boring second. She thought about the horse she had readied for Larame, if things turned south. A bedroll was strapped behind his saddle. She had also hung his gun rig on the saddle, covering it with a long, black, old leather coat that Mark rarely wore. It would be a bit small on Larame, but it would repel the cold wind if he needed. She put some clothes in the saddlebag, and the one hundred dollars she had got from Randy. She had never told him about that, but it would stake him pretty well if he headed to Mexico. The last thing she put in there was the folded paper that was among his things from the Sheriff's Office. He had asked her if she had looked at it, and she had told him "No," and they had left it at that. If it had said "Buddy" on it, she would'a peeked, but for Larame, she allowed him his privacy, like he allowed hers.

She was holding back tears, not hearing any of the business that Randy had brought about missed loans and such.

It was the calling of Larame Crighton to take the stand that perked her back to the present.

The Judge repeated his call. "Will Larame Crighton take the stand?" Buddy was in the front row, but he didn't budge.

"Young man!" the Judge bellowed. "What's your name?"

Buddy stood up and said, "Buddy Col…" and was interrupted by Clint shouting, "That's Buddy Collins, Your Honor! You gotta meet Buddy! He was lost, but I'm the one that found him! I greeted him when he first came into town myself, everyone knows that!"

"Order, order!" The Judge banged his gavel.

"Does anyone here know where Larame Crighton is right now?"

Old Joe raised his hand.

"Oh, just go ahead and speak, Joe. Protocol is busted down to nothin' in this session already. Where the hell is he?"

"He's buried behind the old church, just like I told you last time, Judge. I don't reckon he budged an inch, bein' dead an' all."

"All right, all right, I gotta put an end to all this nonsense. And for this Larame character, I put everything on hold last session, and it seems it got left that way. My peers, and other judges I know, were split fifty-fifty on the topic. Half of them said to hang him, the other half said you can't go hanging a dead man, no matter how good it would make the whole mess seem to come out."

"Now, I figure that if this man right here," again he pointed out Buddy, "ain't Larame Crighton, but is Buddy Collins, and Larame Crighton is buried behind the old church out there, then this court, formal in the name of the Arizona Territory, decides," and he crashed his gavel down real hard and yelled, "Case closed!"

The whole crowd cheered and celebrated, making the Judge sure that he had made the right decision.

Rose held Buddy close to her the whole walk home. Relieved, she cried just as much as if the verdict had gone the other way. When they got to the saloon, Buddy recognized Star. "Hey, Rose, it's Star! Hey, buddy, I'm Buddy!" he laughingly said.

"I know," she said. "Here, help me carry in some of your things."

"My things?" he asked.

"Yes, grab that coat and the gun belt under it, then see if you can carry your bedroll. I'll get your saddlebags."

"You had me all packed up to leave?"

"Yes," she answered, "if the ruling had gone the other way, you would'a had to leave in a flash. I just made sure that you and Star were ready."

She unhooked the boots hanging on Star's side, and they walked into the hotel and saloon, right next to each other.

Buddy said he needed to go do something, and he went outside and mounted Star. He ran him up the street, turned around at the Sheriff's Office, and rode back to the stable. He removed the saddle and cooled Star down, putting him in the stall Lefty had scrawled his name on.

Buddy saw Lefty staggering in and thanked him for taking good care of Star. Lefty mumbled something and collapsed into a pile of hay inside Star's pen.

Larame

Chapter 13

From Good to Bad to Good

That night, Rose arose from the makeshift bed on the floor. It was the middle of the night and she was in a full sweat. She stood up in the hot moonlit night and removed her nightgown. She kicked her makeshift bed to the side, never to be used again. Still glistening, she gazed at the young cowboy's sleeping body. He was naked on her bed. He lay on his back, spread-eagle, with both arms outstretched to each side. Sweat glistened on his muscular body too.

Rose looked at his young, seemingly healed body and marveled at her prior restraint.

Not tonight, she thought, as she climbed onto the bed and lay upon Buddy's body, mirroring his position and shape.

Buddy didn't stir but was fully aware of what was happening as she quietly lowered herself onto him. They kissed, the first real kiss of their time together so far, and she gasped at the fullness of what she suddenly felt.

Slowly they melted together, back and forth, over and over, and the love continued the rest of the night.

The sun, peeking through the open window, and the hunger and thirst in their bodies interrupted their first lovemaking session that following morn. The first light was flickering off his eyes as she lay upon him still and professed her undying love. Buddy looked deep into her eyes and promised his to her.

Rose closed her eyes and silently promised to God that she would never lay with another man, always keeping that promise.

Buddy and Rose went down that long stairway that new morning, laughing and poking and jabbing each other the full way.

They got breakfast together and readied the kitchen and dining tables for the day.

It was after the long lunch crowd was over and before the evening meal that Buddy hugged Rose and whispered in her ear.

"I smell like a dragon," he said. "If it weren't for all that good smell, you rubbed all over me, I'd be scaring off all the customers."

"Bath water in room nine is cold, but pretty well clean still, only been used eight or nine times," she offered.

"I'll take you up on that, and I'll see you before supper," he said before kissing her and heading upstairs.

Rose was polishing silver when she first noticed the commotion out in the street. It wasn't much, but there were some yelling and some horses running past at full gallop, so Rose went to the swinging doors and looked out.

Three young cowboys were racing up and down the street, letting their horses kick a church lady's hat into the wind. Each time she approached it, they galloped by again, kicking it farther away.

She was well dressed, and she wore one of those dresses that made it look like her bottom stuck way up in the air, and the boys weren't used to seeing that, so they had a bit of fun with her.

"Boom!" Everyone turned to see the Sheriff down at the end of the street, holding his smoking six-gun in the air. "Fun's over!" he yelled, and the cowboys quickly pulled their horses up to the saloon.

The church lady picked up her big hat and, while dusting it off, scurried back over to the church grounds.

Meanwhile, the three cowboys, barely more than kids, stood just outside the swinging doors and watched the Sheriff return to his office.

There were maybe ten or twelve customers in the joint at the time the three, burst in. Buddy had hurried his bath and was streaking to the room next door when he heard the first arguing. He listened carefully while dressing, with the door cracked open, making sure things weren't getting out of hand.

He listened carefully and knew what to do.

The young cowboy, the shortest of the three, laid his gun on the bar and spoke directly to Rose. "Now he's already told you that he ain't paying no two dollars for this here bottle of whiskey. He's gonna pay one dollar, and you better get that through your pretty little head!"

"It's two dollars a bottle, boys. Now pay up or mosey on your way."

"You thinkin' you gonna kick us out?" the other little one said. He was the skinniest but looked wiry and was leaning in on Rose with both hands on the bar, trying to make himself look taller.

She pointed at the door, and when she did, some of the customers scurried out whilst the rest of them pinned their own selves up against the wall.

The tall leader had just said, "Now you listin' up, bitch!" when the door to number ten slammed closed.

Everyone, including the three cowboys, looked up to hear "Ching, ching, ching," as he walked down the hall to the stairs. You could have heard a pin drop as Larame Creighton stepped down the first four steps, his Colt .45 strapped low on his left leg.

He didn't say a word as the young leader, a head taller than the others, stepped forward and squared off, showing he had a sidearm as well.

"Smash!" The silence was busted as Joe the undertaker pushed a double-barrel shotgun straight through the window behind them. All three wheeled around to see, only to notice Sheriff Big Jim McGraw push open the swinging doors, one big hand on each. Big Jim stood in the doorway in that exact pose, standing right behind the polished Sheriff's badge pinned on his chest.

"You boys won't be wanting to cause any trouble in my town now, ya hear?" he bellowed. "Least I be marching you over to the jail by your ear."

The tallest now squared to him. "I don't see it working out that way, Sheriff." The little one was starting to tremble, and the other one was sweating bullets when, "Ching!" Larame took another step down the stairs.

I'm not going to have to play a part in this standoff," the Sheriff said boldly.

"I'm thinking we three might just shoot you three, and I'll grab a drink before stepping across your dead body on my way out of town," the young leader spouted.

"Ching!" Larame took another step down, and the leader wheeled and got in his stance to draw.

One was shaking hard now, and the other sweat profusely, as they heard the click of the hammer of the shotgun get armed.

There was a drip of sweat on the young troublemaker's nose, and Rose was watching it to see when it fell.

It fell! No one knows if it even hit the floor, as while that drop of sweat was midair, the young leader slapped leather. Just as his gun cleared his holster, there was an explosion from Larame's Colt, and the punk's gun flew across the room, slamming into the wall right next to Joe.

Joe held his trigger finger still, and the Sheriff just smiled, as one of the troublemakers was lying face down on the floor shaking with his hands and legs outstretched, while the other was standing stiff, facing away from the

Sheriff with his hands and arms outstretched straight up in the air.

The leader stood there in the middle, clutching his bleeding hand, yelling at the top of his lungs, "You motherfucker!" over and over.

No one, even the Sheriff, moved at all as Larame, "Ching! Ching! Ching!" came the rest of the way down the stairs and sat on the last step.

Larame removed his boots and put on his slippers that were waiting there at the bottom of the stairs. He stood up, and everyone watched as Larame then unbuckled his gun belt and re-buckled it in midair, hanging it on the bottom post of the banister. He then took off his hat and placed it on the banister over top of his Colt.

Still, no one moved as he reached over the bar and grabbed his apron and two bar rags.

He put on the apron and handed one of the towels to the bleeding kid, saying, "Yer bleeding all over my clean floor."

He then turned around away from them all and quietly started wiping down tables.

The Sheriff and Joe marched the young would-be outlaws down to the jail, knowing they'd be sitting there near a month until the Judge came back around. Rose, of course, ran out from behind the bar and hugged Buddy for a long time.

Larame

Chapter 14

A Dream Come True

It was mid-fall and the wind had a touch of wood smoke in it as it gently blew by in the street. It wasn't very cold, but it would be soon. The town was bustling with the opening of the church. Seemed the town was blessed with the newcomers and all.

Mark Montpelier was doing well, as was the saloon. Miners had been trickling down almost every day, and he was sending off a strongbox holding gold bars to Laredo and receiving the strongbox back, stuffed with money.

Mark had been taking his cut for the business, but ever since the vaudeville show Rose produced, he had given her all the extra money the hotel and saloon made. She put all that and all the money the girls and Buddy anted up into the kitty.

Mark wasn't too interested in the saloon business anymore as he tended to weighing and melting down gold.

The miners were all happy to visit the saloon for a drink or more and get a fine meal for a change. They mostly only stayed one night but usually used up two girls before heading back up to the mines.

Rose was just flittering about, readying things for the evening, when that fateful day approached from the north, in the back of an old wagon, pulled by an old mule and driven by a grizzled old miner.

No one paid a bit of attention to it, as it slowly made its way toward Yuma, then into the town, pulling up at the Assayer's Office.

The old coot got down and walked to the door and knocked. "Com'on in," Mark yelled at the door.

"No, sir!" came the answer, as the old timer refused to go inside. "You're gonna have to come out here."

The old miner wouldn't take his eyes off that wagon for even a second while holding a sawed-off shotgun at his side.

Mr. Montpelier rushed outside to see the merchandise, and the old miner raised up the tarp enough for Mark to see all the old strongboxes stacked in the back.

"Better call the sheriff over and some deputies," the old guy said.

"You're probably right," and he went over and got Jim and Joe to come see.

The sheriff took one look and sent a young boy to get two more deputies. "Tell 'em to hurry!" he yelled as the boy took off running.

Not even Mark had ever seen that much gold, and they started carrying it inside box after box. Help soon came, and Joe just stood by, holding that shotgun of his, watching the street for anything unusual.

Mark was busy all day, weighing and testing the purity of the gold nuggets and the gold dust, as the sheriff or a deputy was always sitting there watching. Joe was now sitting in a chair just outside the door, still touting that shotgun.

It took all day, but Mark Montpelier, Assayer, finally had a number to give to Jose, the old miner.

Before he told him, Mark went back and opened the safe, walked in, and mostly closed the heavy door. Once inside he started recounting all his money.

He came back outside and looked at the old guy and said, "I'll be giving you eighty thousand dollars for your gold."

"Hold on there, young man!" the old codger erupted. "I've been working most of my whole damn life pulling this gold outta that mountain. I ain't about to let someone cheat me as I cross into the promised land."

"I'm not cheating you, Jose. The truth is, that's all the money I have!" Mark explained.

"Well, it ain't enough! I've been hearing the tales of those miners coming back up the mountain telling that you've been paying them twice what the assayers offer up there."

"That would make it be around one hundred thousand dollars for my gold."

"I don't have one hundred thousand dollars to give you," Mark lamented.

"Well, then you either get it or be hauling my gold back onto that wagon so I can head off to Laredo. I've been doing this my whole life. Don't take me for a fool." The old man stood up and gestured toward the door. "One of us will be passing through there any minute."

"Hang on, I'll go!" Mark jumped up. "I just need to go over to the bank and take out a loan. You wait right here, I'll be back lickety-split, don't you worry none."

Mark ran out the door toward the bank, while the old coot turned and sat, facing the deputy, as they set up the checkerboard on a barrel between them.

Rose had heard some commotion from out in the street, and there were some mumblings during the late breakfast crowd, but she hadn't a clue of what really was going on in town.

Buddy and she were cleaning up and cooking for lunch when the first hints of the deal drifted into the kitchen.

"Big shipment at the Assayer's!" someone said aloud. "Sheriff and his deputies wouldn't all be over there unless it's real big or unless someone broke into Mark's safe, and I seriously doubt the second."

They both heard that said, but neither gave it much thought.

At the bank, Mark Montpelier marched in and excitedly told Randy the whole story. "A lot of money to be made," he hollered, "about a hundred thousand dollars profit alone I figure."

"What's in it for me?" Randy asked the excited assayer.

"Why, a piece of the action, of course!" Mark explained. "All I need you to do is lend me twenty thousand dollars and we'll both make a killing!"

"Twenty thousand? That'll take some paperwork, Mark, and you know it!" Randy countered.

"Well, let's get to it, Randy. The old fart is sitting in my office waiting for me to get back."

Randy brought out some papers and Mark filled them all out.

Randy mulled them all over, then they moved into the back room. Randy sat at his big desk, and Mark was sitting on the couch in the very spot Rose had been so many months before. Remembering that visit like it was yesterday, Randy started shaking his head, saying he couldn't make the deal.

"Gold's too volatile lately," he said.

"What the hell do you mean?" Mark asked.

"It's been going up and down a lot lately," Randy lied.

"It always does that, Randy," Mark explained, "but it goes up a hell of a lot more than it goes down. I staked my life savings on that fact, and this deal will set me up for business just fine."

"Maybe, maybe, but you're dealing with your own money. I'm investing the money of these new church people, and for many of them it's their life savings too. I can't be going back to them saying I lost their money speculating on gold now, can I?"

"Randy, you're a fool!" Mark Montpelier yelled at him, storming out of his office and bank.

Randy waited a few minutes, then excitedly ran over to the saloon to tell

Rose. The whole way over he was thinking about her sitting on that couch again.

Randy got over there, and the excitement was electric. Both Rose and Buddy knew that their plan had just come to pass. Rose hurried up and got the bag of money she had been saving from the safe.

She counted it out and placed it all into her lifted-up apron, and they ran off towards the new Assayer's Office to meet with her boss Mark Montpelier.

Randy went with them, wanting to see what the hell was going on and maybe understand what the plan Rose started so long ago was really all about.

He didn't know about her vow, and he had his visions in his head while wanting to be near Rose and any business that included them both.

Once there, they entered Mark's establishment after Joe opened the door for them. They saw Mark and the old man in a Texas standoff, each one nose to nose, jabbering at each other, sharing nothing new. The checkerboard lay on the floor and the pieces spread all over, while the deputy stood back from the argument waiting on Sheriff McGraw to come bail him out of this mess.

The sheriff followed them in, pushing into the front. "Everybody just calm down!"

And they did.

"I'm sure we can come to a reasonable agreement," he continued.

"Rose? Do you and Buddy have business here today with the assayer?" he asked politely.

"Yes, we do!" she answered.

"You do?" Mark said, astonished.

"Yes!" she answered again, dumping all the money from her apron onto his big mahogany desk. "Ten thousand, one hundred- and twenty-two-dollars' worth of business."

"Make that ten thousand two hundred and twenty-two," Buddy said as he dropped the one-hundred-dollar bill he had found in his saddlebags into the pile.

The old miner watched and his eyes lit up, wondering if that big pile of money would soon be his.

"You hardly come over to the hotel at all anymore, Mark," Rose exclaimed. "Your time is all taken up over here with this gold. I've been running the place for quite some time, and even you know that business has improved because of my work."

"Here's what I say," she continued. "You give this good man his eighty thousand dollars for his wholly owned gold, then we'll add in this little over ten thousand to the big pile, long as you sign over the deed to the hotel to me and the girls."

Mark looked up and said, "It's worth way over twice that, Rose!"

"Quiet, Mark, I ain't done yet proposing this here deal!"

Mark sat down and she continued. "Next you have to write up papers promising to put another ten thousand dollars in this poor miner's name into the bank for saving. That'll make it a good deal for him, even a bit more than he was asking.

"You'll be making a profit by sending the purified gold to Laredo, so the tired old guy doesn't have to keep hauling it around."

"Sure, I'll be having a good deal too, just like everybody else here, as Randy makes some sure-fire money on the saving deal too," the sheriff, and Deputy Joe, the undertaker, Mark and Buddy will all attest and sign the papers making this miner a guarantee like no other that he'll be getting his last ten grand soon enough!

"Now, if we can all agree on this deal, we can quit arguing and start celebrating over at my new saloon!"

Everybody looked at each other and then to Jose the miner, and he finally broke the silence.

"That their pretty lady sure knows how to spin up a yarn!" he said with a smile. "Sure, I'll be taking that deal if you all agree too!"

Everyone started shaking each other's hands, and soon all the papers were signed, and the old miner scooped all of Rose's money up into a bag, and on the way to the saloon yelled out, "Drinks are on me!"

Larame

Chapter 15

Lefty

Everyone knew it was Rose that pulled off the biggest deal that had ever hit Yuma, but she was the only one that knew it was Buddy's idea and plan.

The girls walked down the street, even past the church, with their heads held high, widely known as the owners and not the ladies of the night that they had previously been. Everyone, including the other shopkeepers, now tipped their hats and greeted them good morning with respect.

Their new roles and attitudes helped Rose's Morningstar Hotel and Saloon get even more famous and busy.

"They wanted a smaller sign over at the church," she explained to Buddy. The men were there with the new sign, and she explained to them just what she wanted.

"You put that big new oval sign that says Rose's right up there on the top left side, angled a bit to accentuate its importance, right by the big M in Morningstar," she instructed.

"Put that great big bouquet of roses sign, behind the main sign so it sticks way out of both the top and bottom of the sign. Make it on the same angle as the Rose's sign."

"Lastly, place all those single roses around the whole sign, framing all in, and the rest of them scattered all over the front of the building."

She looked over at the plain square rather small sign across the street that read, "New Church of Christ, all are welcome," and laughed. "They should have shook my hand that day!"

Rose wasn't helping matters, and the church ladies made some selfish demands, trying to get her saloon pushed out of town. They had built a huge beautiful church and their design and building skills were first rate, so they proposed a luxury hotel with a new ballroom just down the street.

Their proposal didn't go through when the judge came through, but he was so upset with all the petty issues and proposals from the new people that he demanded they make some sort of governing body for the town of Yuma.

They decided on a mayor and council.

The next week, the preacher threw his hat into the ring for mayor, and the sheriff, seeing that, decided to run too.

Everyone figured the sheriff would win, but the preacher had everyone's ear and was whipping up a frenzy, demanding votes to save the town.

The sheriff started to get criticized for some past actions, and he didn't like the dirty mess he was in, so when a group of people inserted Buddy Collins's name into the hat, Big Jim bowed out and gave his support to Buddy.

Buddy wasn't interested in the job but told the people that came in he would serve the town fairly if elected.

It was doubtful he would win until a deacon in the church, feeling he'd been shorted by the preacher and other leadership, decided to run too.

He was right, and a lot of the church folk knew it, and he garnered their support.

The pastor quickly made plans to oust him after he won the election, and that plan leaked.

After the election votes were counted later that week, Buddy had won by a landslide. The numbers showed that almost half of the church folk voted for Buddy, unhappy with the corruption the race had uncovered in their leadership.

A new pastor was sent into town by the head church, and the deacon was admonished for tarnishing the church.

The word was they were strictly forbidden to enter any politics until they got approval from above.

Buddy took the job in stride. Everybody liked Buddy, and he even spoke at the church, promising to keep their issues in his mind and heart. They liked that, and for as much as they seemed to hate Rose, they were actually quite fond of Buddy.

Buddy solved the disputes fairly. He listened to each side equally. He agreed with a lot of things said on both sides, never making anyone look small. When people lost a decision to their opponent, Buddy would console them, giving them pointers and help on how to do better if there was a next time.

Buddy did hate one group in town. That was bullies and anyone who came into town to cause trouble. He would always turn those individuals over to Sheriff McGraw.

Winter was setting in, and they got word from the judge that since they had a new mayor, and since he trusted Big Jim, unless there was a murder or something big, he wouldn't be coming back till spring.

Things went real smooth with Buddy and the sheriff in charge.

The saloon and hotel weren't as busy as the miners that had been coming down for the winter pretty much petered out.

Winters down in Yuma were short and not as cold as up north, but it dipped down low at night, and next August would show a significant rise in births for the year.

It was one of those cold nights that Buddy went out to check on Star.

When he opened the stall, he started crying. He fell down upon Star, who was lying flat on the ground, and held his dead friend's head in his arms. Star had been trying to keep old Lefty warm and alive, but it turned out he failed. Lefty was dead.

He dusted Lefty off and laid him down on the floor of the stall proper. He took Star into the next stall and put Star's blanket on Lefty to cover him up.

He ran and told Rose. As she ran to the stable, he went quickly and woke up Jim and Joe.

He went to tell Clint and Terrence, who were both known to befriend him, and they all met in the stable with Rose crying, holding Lefty's head to her breast.

The funeral the next day was sparse. Lefty was a drunk and worthless to most people that didn't get to know him. No one from the new church bothered to come, and they didn't want Lefty to be the first person buried behind their new church.

Joe the undertaker led the procession of Lefty's friends behind the old church, and they buried Lefty not far from the marker that said, "Here Lies Larame Crighton."

The Death and Life of Larame Crighton

Larame

Chapter 16

Yuma, Center of the Southwest

Spring was a welcome sight in Yuma. There wasn't much greenery except in spring, and the gentle rains washed the dirty place clean again for the year.

The whole town was prospering, but not as much as the Assayer's Office and Rose's Morningstar Hotel and Saloon.

Girls came from all over to work, and Rose worked out some great vaudeville acts for them to play-act on Friday and Saturday nights. By mid-summer, real acts started to show up, and on Wednesdays, people would come from miles around to pack the joint to the ceiling.

Signs and posters were everywhere, on most of the shops, showing the coming attractions.

Buddy and Rose prospered.

All the while, the ballroom at the new church remained mostly empty.

The years passed and the town grew. The church finally got their mayor and had pushed new ordinances through. They couldn't directly attack Rose's business, but they were slowly but surely pushing it out, and Rose got too tired of fighting with them.

Buddy saw her unhappiness day after day and made plans to sell out to none other than Mark Montpelier.

Mark wanted to be part of the stardom and rub shoulders with some of the stars that came to town to do their show. He figured he could influence the mayor to relax some of the new restrictions if he eliminated the prostitution and just continued the rest of the debauchery.

He ended up wrong, of course, but the stardom was well worth the price to him, and he spent some of his vast fortune bringing in the best and most gay of all the traveling performances.

Buddy and Rose packed up and headed for Nevada, where the rules were said to be a lot looser.

Half the summer went by there, and they became more and more convinced that while it was completely legal in the state, the government was closing the noose on any new establishments.

The rules Rose would have to follow were far too strict, and they had built in clauses for even more restrictions and stiffer penalties. Buddy refused to sign, and they proceeded to go further east.

Rose was sure that it was west they should go, figuring it was wilder and more lawless there, but Buddy disagreed and kept going east.

Buddy had spent most of the day talking to this flamboyant character that had a lewd act featuring two men, but one dressed as a woman. The act entailed them meeting on the street, complete with a cardboard set. It showed how they went on a whirlwind affair, falling deeply in love. And on every change of scenery, one or the other would disrobe the other just a little bit more.

The last scene showed the man's bare ass, naked and exposed to all, and the presumed beautiful girl, her huge breasts on display, wearing only her panties, dropped her drawers, revealing his huge manhood dangling between his legs.

The crowd gasped, and the makeshift curtains quickly closed on the show.

They had their buggy packed and ready to go in the event that the law burst in and tried to arrest them, and they waited in the shadows for the reaction of the crowd.

One person started to clap, and immediately the applause and roars became thunderous.

The actors returned for an encore, and the curtain opened and closed, exposing the two naked men, one always turned away from the crowd and facing the beautiful and busty girl-man, with his massive tool swaying back and forth between his or her legs.

Open and closed, again and again, to the delight of the crowd. They received a thunderous applause every time.

That buggy was not needed, and a stagehand took it back to the stable, as Mark met the two participants backstage and invited them to his new mansion on the edge of town.

Buddy had listened intently the whole day before that show, as the men explained they had been performing on a nightly basis and had concocted and worked out all the kinks to their show in New Orleans.

He listened as they explained how the Canal Street rules differed from the rules of the city. These unwritten rules seemed to perfectly fit Rose's unusual attitude and demeanor.

They had invited Buddy and Rose to join them in New Orleans. They even proposed that they would help if they ever came to visit or stay.

He continued driving the Conestoga wagon east towards his goal, refusing to discuss his idea, lest it be all a lie.

Rose took the empty time and the quiet night to get Buddy to open up about his past.

Larame

Chapter 17

Diary of a Young Outlaw

Reluctant at first, when he finally started talking about his past, the stories started flowing like water.

Larame Crighton had experienced a tattered life as a child and young man. He never complained or spoke of it, but he was teased and poked unmercifully for his stutter in school and at play.

His speech was so hard to listen to that often people would nonchalantly walk away from him in mid-sentence. He heard "Spit it out!" so often that he did just that and habitually spit all the time, even indoors. They got him in even more hot water, but he just couldn't stop.

That stutter and spitting likely came from his treatment at home. Larame's father seemed to like nothing more than to beat him, then go make violent love to his mom.

He beat young Larame every time something went wrong during the day at his job, and things were always going wrong, getting him in hot water.

Larame had welts growing on top of the welts from the last episode, and every time he got beat his mom got fucked hard. She tended to ignore most of the fighting and screaming from his room, telling Larame to try to do better and to do something nice for his Pa, and she hoped that part of the sex would someday go away.

Larame loved his mom with all his heart anyway. He didn't say it to Rose, but he figured that was one of the many reasons he had for loving her so much, even though she carried a torrid past.

Larame got to the part about when he met Cliff Williams the next night.

He had met Cliff at a bar, and Cliff, a few years older than Larame, had remembered him from brief school days. Cliff had quit early and was following his dreams. He was the kind of guy always talking about tomorrow, and things he was going to do, and never talked about yesterday or any of the misfortunes of the past. Larame hung on all of Cliff's words and admired him, holding him up as if he was his big brother. Cliff treated him like a brother too, and soon they were inseparable, pulling pranks and getting in fights, always laughing and heading for the next adventure.

One day they robbed a store. They snuck in and snuck out without being seen and escaped hiding behind the very store they had just robbed. They split the twenty-six dollars they stole and sucked on the candy they threw into the bag.

The sheriff came around during the fuss, and no one in the entire area suspected the two young men in the crowd.

That night they were still celebrating with drinks at the saloon when they watched Larame's father get up and go home, staggering drunk.

"Watch this," Cliff whispered. "You stay here!" as Cliff got up and followed the drunk father into the alley.

Larame moved to the small window and watched as Cliff jumped him. He punched him and kicked him, leaving him moaning, and was on his way back into the bar as the old man crawled off to his home.

Larame never felt either sadness or glee over what he watched that night, but the image was burned into his brain. Seeing his father crawling on his knees, crying out for help, was how he'd picture him from now on, erasing the vision of the strong villainous master he so hated in his youth.

Larame then reached into the saddlebag he had been using for a pillow at night. He pulled out an old folded paper. Rose recognized it right away and watched as he slowly opened it up. He looked at it long and hard before turning it and sharing it with Rose. In his hands was a wanted poster that said Wanted, Dead or Alive, and a hand-drawn picture of a handsome young cowboy. Tears filled Rose's eyes in the darkness of that wagon as she read the bottom because it said Cliff Williams.

"I knew what I was getting into," Buddy said softly.

"Maybe it was because it was too easy," Buddy continued, not realizing her deep sorrow, or maybe that young churchgoing Larame needed a brother. Whatever the case, he listened carefully as Cliff explained their next plan.

"Don't worry," he told Larame. "Just follow along. I did this before up in Castle Dome City over a year ago. We'll be in Mexico living it up, and you won't have to wonder about your father or nobody ever again."

The next morning, Larame, riding Star, followed along behind Cliff and his horse Spank. They tied up at the rail right outside the bank while most of the townspeople were still asleep.

Randy was not asleep, having just opened the bank, and was propped up reading the paper in the only window of the bank open for business, when the two young outlaws burst into the bank demanding all the money.

Randy was trembling and stuttering as he agreed and took the saddlebag down under the counter, opened the locker, and stuffed the money into the bag.

"All of it!" Cliff demanded, and Randy reached behind and opened a small drawer and pulled out more money. Stuffing it in with the other, he slammed the full saddlebag onto the counter while pulling the trigger on the single-shot shotgun pointed right at the boys under the counter.

The blast went right through the wall and hit young Larame, right in the guts. Pieces of wood went flying as Randy crawled down under the counter, trembling and scared. Cliff threw the saddlebag over his shoulder and with the other hand grabbed Larame's collar, assisting him back onto the street. Larame was wide-eyed in shock, leaning against Star, and somehow got a foot in the stirrup and held onto the saddle horn as Star took off following Spank at a full run.

They ran like that for hours, Star's reins dragging on the ground the whole time, and Larame was frozen in place, just hanging on.

It was when they stopped for rest that young Larame fell off of Star, as his hat fell onto the ground.

"Help me back up on Star," Larame pleaded.

Cliff noticed a small bird place a piece of straw inside the upside-down hat.

"You're a goner," Cliff told him. "God damn it, your boot knows you're a goner, your shirt knows you're a goner, even the little fucking bird knows your time's up."

He paused and then continued, "Seems you're the only one here that doesn't know it."

"I gotta go now!" he scowled. "Don't be thinking I stole your horse. If it means anything, you were a good friend, and I'll miss you, and I hate leaving you like this. I gotta go now!"

"Giddy-up!" he yelled, and spurred Spank into a full run.

Larame looked up at Rose, and his sad eyes turned bright again. "That's when I found you!" he smiled. "Turns out to be the best day of my life."

Rose's eyes welled all up, and she hugged him tight. They laid in the back of that old wagon in the moonlight and made soft love.

Turned out to be just another of the many best days of both of their lives.

Larame

Chapter 18

New Orleans

They drove that Conestoga wagon pulled by two big mules and followed by Star tied to the rear, right into New Orleans. They followed the trolley tracks south, down towards the Gulf, and he pulled up at the main street in the French District. Buddy looked around, standing up, looking for something he'd know when he saw it. There, not far to his right, was the spot he was looking for.

He drove the wagon across the tracks into the dingy part of town with all the warehouses, wagons, and men loading from the docks in the south, and the factory area to the north.

He pulled the wagon into the open lot that separated that bustle from the area the tourists flocked to each day.

The trolley was loud at times and stopped right at the street. It was late, and they got ready to sleep, raising the white cloth roof not from the weather, but from any unknown danger in this strange town.

Rose lay beside Buddy and asked, "Are you sure we can park here for the night?"

"I might just be thinking to park here the rest of our lives," he answered.

"Isn't it about time you tell me the things you seem to know?" she pleaded.

"All I can say for sure is that I do have a plan," was his answer.

Rose perked up at those words. "I just love a good plan, Buddy!"

"I know, Rose, I know that for sure, but you'll have to wait till morning, to give me a chance to see if my plan even gets off the ground. What I will tell you is, I know the owner of this place we're parked at, and I hope to be sleeping with the new owner if my plan comes to play out true."

Rose snuggled up next to Buddy and they slept unbothered, right after the last trolley clanged past for the night.

The next morning saw Buddy kiss Rose goodbye and start walking down Canal Street towards the French Quarter.

Rose straightened the mess in the wagon, then set her sights on the vacant lot. She scurried around picking up trash and piling up old lumber.

With the help of some old bums that were lingering around, smelling the stew she was cooking, she put up a big tent, and was fixing the insides up when Buddy returned.

"Deals done!" he said excitedly. "This is our place now. They wouldn't take any money for it, just hoping we help them out if we can."

Where everyone else saw the disgusting start of a skid row, filled with warehouses, Buddy and Rose saw a gold nugget.

Buddy staked out that empty lot and hired the construction of a huge new building designed to be just like Rose's Morningstar Hotel and Saloon, only bigger and better.

It sat sideways to the street, aimed across the tracks and facing the French Quarter's beautiful architecture. Placed just like that to block most of the sight of the goings-on behind the building.

It went up fast as Buddy directed the construction. He had learned a lot helping build the Assayer's Office in Yuma and had made improvements to the Yuma Saloon, one being that the balcony was now almost fifteen feet wide, and the stairs widened as well. The design included plenty of rooms, with the biggest and best on the bottom floor right behind the kitchen, reserved for Rose and Buddy alone.

The balcony was to make shows more appealing and bigger than life.

He built the hotel to be beautiful on the inside and outside, just like his Rose.

When it was finished, it was truly beautiful and could be seen for a good distance, but they still awaited the sign. When it came down the street, all the carriages had to be averted because of its great size and shape.

The huge star was raised up by ropes from the roof as it was placed on the scaffolding high above the building. It was just a huge yellow star, and the only lettering was "STAR" in great big letters.

You could see that sign as far as you could see, from down on Canal Street.

Star, of course, was in the large stable behind the building, designed to handle all the customers' buggies and horses.

Hearing about the new openings and jobs, the young girls from all over gathered at Rose's feet. She taught them her ways, showing them the difference from a whore and a lady. A whore gives them sex, she would always repeat. We give them love, and we keep giving them our love and we mean it from in our hearts. Ain't none of you girls gonna be whores, she would tell them over and over.

"You will walk down that street with your heads held up high, knowing that plenty of the men walking around love you and your new sisters. Don't be discouraged by the church ladies, all scrunched up and proud. They're usually all filled with hate and are most likely secretly jealous."

She trained them well, and the prettiest and most coordinated she taught to dance.

Buddy would take them down to the French Quarter's strip clubs and secure them jobs, complete with well-being. No one mistreated Buddy and Rose's girls, and all the club owners were in Buddy's debt.

Buddy walked down that street often and was soon well known. His long, soft, baby-fine hair turned prematurely white, and he grew a big white beard, making him a recognizable sight.

The old wound in his side caused him a lot of pain during these long walks, and he stopped to rest often and stayed seated a long bit.

During these rests, Buddy was painted over and over by the street artists as they waited for a client. They sold those pictures to the shops for food and board money as they struggled to get noticed for a real artist's job.

Soon his picture hung everywhere, and he was made the honorary mayor of Canal Street, even leading the parade one Mardi Gras, also known as Fat Tuesday.

The shows they put on up on that balcony didn't raise the amount of attraction they had hoped and were soon canceled. There were just too many finely crafted shows around to be upended by the amateurish efforts they were making.

Buddy used that failure to turn it into their biggest, most profitable attraction.

Buddy put tables and chairs up there in front of every door, and they rented the new luxury rooms to the rich and famous when they visited town. From then on, the back stairs were used by everyone else, including any services for any of the guests.

Right there on the edge, hiding the skid row, was a place for the rich and famous to be treated like the stars they were. Right there under the Star.

Buddy and Rose made their fortune owning and running the Star. Everyone loved and admired Buddy, and all the young girls looked up to Rose. Many a great career was started here by mixing the pretty and talented young girls with the rich and influential people that attended the Star.

Buddy's initial friends were doing just as well over at the other end of Canal Street. Buddy visited them often too. He would introduce them to the young men that wouldn't allow themselves to be called homos. They took all those boys in, quickly teaching them the ropes.

We could leave it all there, them in paradise, in Paradise, New Orleans, but Rose took sick.

The cancer ravaged her insides, leaving her appearance still as pretty as silk pajamas. It only took two weeks, and she was gone.

Larame

Chapter 19

Rose

That evening Buddy gave the Star to all the girls and the two boys working there. Equal shares, they all owned the best spot on the strip.

He then took Rose in a finely made casket back to Yuma in a buckboard pulled by those two mules, and followed again by Star.

He made a deal at the Pony Express to insert his buckboard in one of their runs, giving them the two mules in the deal.

They agreed, and Buddy on Star followed Rose across the desert, all the way to Yuma.

There were cheers and big smiles whenever they saw Buddy's face, but the celebration went cold when they saw the fine casket and realized that Buddy had not returned alone.

Joe the undertaker cried out loud first, followed by Jim and the rest.

Joe laid her out in the street, opening the casket for everyone to see. He touched her up some, but her beauty didn't need much as she laid there, eyes closed as if she was asleep.

Buddy sat there with her all that night. The sheriff sat there too, and old Joe. They were joined that night by Terrence, and soon Grace and her new husband Clint. Matt was there, and the barrel maker, Henry. Even Randy from the bank was there, hanging back, but with the others, their heads hanging low.

Lola and Dolly were there all night too, along with all the other girls from the saloon.

Even the church ladies made a fuss in their own way. They rang the bell all morning and had a sermon on love and acceptance. They didn't attend the burial though.

They started the procession at first light, everybody already present. And they slowly marched out behind the old church, to the slow banging of a drum.

It was one of the two boys that had saw her bare ass, and they hung their heads as they followed the group, him banging slowly on the drum and his younger brother playing a flute, real soft.

There was a great number of hysterics, and loud wailing and crying, as they all dropped armfuls of roses from the nearby field onto her casket in the grave. It was near full when they said the prayers, and started to silently fill in her grave, the dirt clods not making a sound.

Most stayed there for over an hour before drifting off, with Buddy, Joe, and the Sheriff being last to leave. They soon headed off for the saloon to give one last toast to the girl they all loved.

Buddy built a house there in Yuma, on the other side of town from the church people. He lived there happily, taking on the job of Deputy and spending his days in the Sheriff's Office for the next few years, while visiting Rose every day.

The Death and Life of Larame Crighton

Larame

Chapter 20

Cliff Williams

Cliff Williams was living in a small town in Mexico. The money he had stolen had run out a long time ago, but with the last of it, he had bought some land and an orchard growing fruit.

He made a fair living off that orchard, but it was hard work and he was bored of it all.

He kept thinking and dreaming of becoming rich and knew this old orchard wasn't ever going to get him where he dreamed, he'd like to be.

He couldn't get his plan to go back up to the Arizona Territory and rob another bank out of his head.

One day, he saddled up Spank and took off north. He was just outside Yuma as the sun started to come out, as he told himself, I'll just do the same thing as before.

He walked Spank through the sleeping town and hitched his horse up to the rail. He calmly walked into the bank and up to the counter, catching Randy off guard this early in the day.

"How can I help you?" Randy asked, not recognizing him at first.

"Give me all your money!" Cliff yelled, suddenly changing his demeanor and pointing his gun at Randy's face.

"Sure, sure!" Randy responded, filling the saddlebags once again and remembering where he saw that face before. Right when he placed the saddlebags on the counter, that shotgun "BOOM" blew out the wall again, but this time Cliff was ready for that trick and had moved out of the way.

Wood splinters still hitting him, Cliff busted his way back behind the counter and shot Randy in his left leg as he was hiding under the counter. Then Cliff shot him again, saying, "That one's for Larame. I should shoot you in the guts instead of the legs for what you did to him!"

Cliff then ran out the door just as the Sheriff was waking up Buddy.

"It was him again!" Randy cried out to the Sheriff and all the Deputies that were forming a posse. The new church doctor in town started to attend him and pushed back the crowd.

The posse took off to the north following the trail, but Big Jim stopped Buddy, saying, "Buddy, you follow me!"

Buddy followed the Sheriff going full speed to the west instead of following the tracks north with the posse.

Buddy didn't know it, but they beat Cliff Williams back to that Mission. They tied their horses to the rail there and went inside.

Cliff was running hard when he crossed the border to Mexico. The posse, realizing they were beat, returned to Yuma empty-handed.

Now if Cliff was alert, when he hitched up his horse, he would have recognized Star hitched right next to Spank.

Cliff wasn't looking at horses. He had his eyes set on seeing that preacher and yelling, "I give myself up to Jesus!" one last time. He walked into the empty church and hollered for the preacher. "Anybody home?" he yelled.

His answer came in the form of "Click! Click!" as the Sheriff and Buddy stood up from behind that counter, each pointing a Colt 45 at his head.

Cliff looked up, too surprised to recognize Buddy, looked straight at the Sheriff, saying, "Listen here, Sheriff, you have no jurisdiction here. I'm in Mexico!"

"Maybe you are at the moment, but we'll see about that in a minute or two," the Sheriff answered, as he spun a fifty-dollar gold piece onto the counter. It was still spinning when the pastor of that mission scurried out and snatched it up, dropping it in the collection plate in one smooth motion. He had his back to Cliff as the two men marched Cliff, walking backward all the way, fifty feet, back into Arizona Territory.

"Yer under arrest for the robbing and the shooting of poor Randy at the Bank of Yuma! You understand me?" the Sheriff told him. "Buddy, go get all our horses."

"Hey," Cliff yelled, "you called him your buddy. He ain't your friend. Why, he's my friend, Larame Crighton. I'd know that face anywhere!"

"Meet Buddy Collins, my Deputy," the Sheriff said as he disarmed Cliff.

Buddy returned with the horses, and Cliff asked him full out, "What the hell's going on here, Larame?"

Buddy didn't answer as he held his gun pointed directly at Cliff. The Sheriff got on his horse first, holding Spank's reins tight and letting Spank know it, while Buddy and Cliff mounted up. They hadn't traveled far at all before Cliff gave need of a break and quickly pulled a gun out of his boot and pointed it right at the Sheriff.

Big Jim started to draw and clutch his chest both at the exact same time. His gun had barely cleared his holster as it dropped onto the ground, and a few seconds later the Sheriff tipped off the old horse and joined his gun with a thud.

"I didn't shoot him, Larame. I never pulled the trigger!" Cliff shouted, as Larame just looked on in amazement.

"I know," Larame started to answer, when the Sheriff's old horse turned a bit to take a bite of grass at Star's feet. Just as he pulled out that grass, he shit all over the dead Sheriff's legs.

Cliff was watching as if in slow motion when a little bird landed on the Sheriff's hat, now laying on the ground, and placed a piece of straw into the large opening.

"What the hell's going on here?" Cliff said aloud.

"Don't know. I think the Sheriff had a heart attack and died!" Larame Crighton answered.

Larame checked Big Jim and, yes, he was stone cold dead.

"Help me get him up on his horse," Larame pleaded.

"You ain't still thinking of taking me in, are you? Why, the only person I've done any harm to in my whole life was to shoot the legs of the asshole that shot you in the guts!"

"Just get down here and help me," Larame said again.

They tried nearly an hour to get Big Jim back on that horse, but they couldn't do it, try as they may.

They sat there staring at the dead Sheriff's body when Cliff asked Larame a question. "You have any information about my sister Rose back there in Yuma?"

"Your sister?" Larame asked.

"Yeah," he answered, "last I knew she worked at the Morningstar."

"Yeah, I know who you're talking about," Larame said. "She's doing just fine. I think she's still working at the saloon there in town."

"Larame, you tell her I miss her and that I love her. Okay?"

"I'll be sure to do that for you; I talk to her bout every day."

"No shit!" Cliff said, seeming amazed.

"You know she's an Angel, don't you, Cliff?"

"Oh, she was always an angel, Larame."

At that moment, the Sheriff's old horse laid down on the ground beside the dead body.

They quickly got up and pulled the body across the horse's back and coaxed the old horse back up to its feet. Big Jim stayed on his back and they got back on their horses. This time it was Larame clutching the Sheriff's horse's reins tight in his palm.

The two outlaws sat there, both on their horses, looking at each other, wondering what to do.

It was Larame that broke the stalemate.

"If it means anything, you've been a good friend, and I thank you for being my brother. I hate to leave you like this, but I have to go now. You take care," and he threw the saddlebag to Cliff, saying, "Giddy-up!"

Buddy Collins rode one way, returning to Yuma, while Cliff Williams rode the other, into Mexico.

The End

TWISTED TRUTH PRESS